MONICA'S SECRET

Erogenous Zones: Book One

Saskia Walker

MONICA'S SECRET
Erogenous Zones: Book One

First published in 2010

Cover design by Frauke Spanuth at Croco Designs.

MONICA'S SECRET

Chapter One

Just one touch would do it—one deliberate stroke of her fingers over the ornate brass door handle and Monica would see and feel it all, every lust-filled moment that had gone on inside that room, every breathtaking seduction. The residual sexual energy on the door handle was electric, and when she'd first felt it she'd pulled back. It was a risky indulgence to explore it at work, it always was. As the housekeeping manager at Cumbernauld's of Kensington, she didn't want any of the hotel staff to find out about her rather peculiar psychic skill with objects and their sexual history. However, there wasn't anyone around, and it had been a long time since Monica had indulged herself, so she was tempted.

Tentatively, she trailed her fingers down the paneled door of the hotel suite. The lingering vitality from the night before presented her with sudden, intoxicating images of a couple who were about to make love. Sexual energy pulsed up her arm, rapidly opening up an array of erotic images in her mind.

The couple had laughed as they returned to their room, stopping every few feet for open-mouthed kisses, hands roving each other eagerly. The woman had faced the door expectantly while her lover pulled the cardkey from his pocket. Before he unlocked the door, he shoved her body against the surface of the door roughly, and the woman groaned with pleasure. He pushed his cock hard against her bottom while he told her exactly what he was going to do to her.

Going to make you beg. He'd whispered the promise against her ear while he pulled her short skirt up around her hips, right there in the hotel corridor. She wasn't wearing panties, and she was exposed in a public place. Unsettled, but even more aroused, the woman had glanced quickly along the corridor. A loud moan escaped her and she wriggled frantically against the door when he stroked the edge of the cardkey over her bared buttock, scratching the surface of her tender skin, readying her for what was to come.

Monica jerked back and stared at the door. Intrigued, she glanced up and down the corridor. Somewhere far beyond she heard a vacuum and Josie, the housekeeper for this floor, singing, as she often did as she worked. It was okay, she hadn't been drawn in for too long.

Startled at the intensity of the experience and instantly aroused, she put one hand to her chest to level herself, closing her eyes for a moment in order to pull back. This was Monica's gift, this was her burden—she saw and felt the erotic history of objects, imbued as they were with the sexual energy of the people who had handled them. Memories captured in time raced through her from the point of contact, memories that were specifically erotic. This one was powerful. She'd barely made contact with the door. But they'd been right up against it, and it was often this way if the relationship that lingered had been particularly passionate, offering a secondary experience that was both delicious—and her own private form of torture. At her fingertips, she had a personal stash of mystery erotic experiences, a gift that filled her with desire and excitement, but also left her lonely and aching.

"Hey, Monica. Thanks for coming down. I picked up some lost property for your collection."

She glanced away to where Josie had stuck her head out of the next suite along the corridor. Josie had called her to check out the suite before it was made over for the next guests, citing low-level damage that warranted repairs, but no customer charges.

"Check these out." Josie winked and held up a pair of handcuffs. They flashed diamante in the sunlight that came from the window at the end of the hallway.

Handcuffs. Monica clutched her electronic notepad against her side as she walked steadily along the thickly carpeted hallway towards Josie.

"I would have given them to you later," Josie commented, as she observed the way the cuffs glinted in the light, "but these look pretty genuine to me, like…they're worth a bit, you know?" Josie's eyes widened as she studied the gem-studded cuffs.

Monica nodded. "Yes, of course. You did the right thing, I'm sure the owner will realize they left them behind pretty soon. I'll log the item right way so that reception is aware I've got them if they ask at the front desk."

She opened her notepad and wrote on the screen, noting the time of collection and the suite number. It was her responsibility as housekeeping manager to secure valuable lost property until it was claimed, but an item such as this would be extremely difficult for her to handle, laden as it would be with sexual energy. It was specifically sexual energy that her psychic ability tapped. Why, she had no clue, and she'd never been able to talk to anyone besides her sisters about it, for fear of being branded a freak. Their grandmother had been psychic, and Monica and her sisters had inherited it from her, but her grandmother's skill had nothing to do with sex, and Monica's was all to do with sex. She could block it out, but after she'd experienced part of the story by the door, her curiosity was up about the rest, and she didn't trust herself not to make a slip in front of Josie.

Taking the cuffs quickly, she pushed them into her jacket pocket then focused on her electronic notebook to distract herself from the heat and energy contained in the object. Even so, she felt it through the lining of her jacket, the gem-studded cuffs resting heavily against her hipbone.

"Thank you, Josie, I'll make some notes on the condition of the suite and you can get in there and be done for the day." She mustered a smile, and nodded at Josie. "How's hubby?" she added, as a distraction from the seductive call the object in her pocket had on her.

Josie rolled her eyes. "You know what men are like. Honestly, you'd think a broken leg was the end of the world."

Monica chuckled. She lived alone, but the comment made her think of her dad. "I bet he's glad of the company when you get home after work."

"Too right. He's missing work and his workmates, and I think that's been a learning experience in itself." Josie winked.

Monica could tell Josie was secretly enjoying the unusual home situation, even while she wondered what a usual home situation was. Monica's parents had a pretty normal setup, because her mother's generation had skipped the psychic stuff that Monica and her sisters had inherited from the family line. That was the closest Monica knew to normal.

When Josie went back to her work, Monica let out a withheld breath. She was aroused by what she'd felt and didn't want Josie to notice anything out of the ordinary. Monica kept her psychometrics a secret, which was not only hard but forced a lonely life on her. When she wanted to open to it, however—as she did today—it was a ticket to ride on the residual sexual energy left behind on physical objects. Returning her attention to the suite, she used her master cardkey on the door and opened herself fully to what lingered there.

Flipping the lock on the door to ensure her privacy, she pressed the cuffs inside her jacket pocket against her hip as she walked across the room. The nerve endings in her palm and along her flank vibrated expectantly. The room was filled with a heavily seductive aura. How could she resist?

The suite was top end, one of the most luxurious in the hotel with a Hollywood nostalgia theme. Art deco furnishings in the sitting room led on to a bedroom featuring a massive round bed with a black lacquered headboard. A peaches and black color scheme was carried throughout.

In the bedroom, Monica ran one finger along the dresser and saw the man standing there. The fleeting image of him revealed a polished, brutish-looking man, a man who was confident in his sexuality. He wore a leather jacket over a white shirt. His head was shaved, but for a zig-zag line of hair on one side that served to show off the attractive shape of his skull. Power oozed from his every pore.

There was a self-assured flicker in his eyes as he lifted something from the dresser. A hairbrush. He smacked the back of the brush against his palm as if testing it, then turned to where the woman Monica had sensed by the door was crawling across the floor on her hands and knees, as if headed for the bed. She glanced back at him with an expectant and mischievous look in her eyes.

Monica's core clenched, heat traversing her entire skin as the woman reached back and lifted the hem of her skirt, pulling it up and over her hips, once more revealing her naked bottom to her man. From where he stood, he could see her glistening wet slit. The woman was aroused, and now Monica was too.

The man walked closer, and with the toe of one of his polished boots he nudged her knees further apart, making her display herself even more. The woman moaned and shifted on her knees until her thighs were wider. She let her head hang down as if she was ashamed by her exposure. It was a decadent sense of shame though, an entirely relished experience. After a moment admiring the view, the man squatted down behind her, and ran his fingers between the damp folds of her pussy.

He told her how naughty she was, then ran the back of the hairbrush over her buttock. The woman shivered expectantly. He landed the hairbrush on her pale buttock several times in quick succession, and when he paused her buttock had developed a rosy hue, the niche of her sex glistening even more. He turned his attention to the other buttock. Monica's core tightened as she imagined what that must feel like, knowing it was coming and wanting it. The image faded.

Monica stepped quickly across the room, chasing after it. It was then that she noticed the black lacquered headboard was marked with a small dent and a scratch. It was the damage that Josie had reported. Monica smiled as she guessed what might have made the mark. Her hand went to her jacket and she rested it over the shape of the cuffs. Yes, he'd pinned her cuffed wrists up there while he teased her nipples with the other hand.

Unable to resist, she ran her hands over the headboard. The images moved fast through her mind. The woman had laid here naked and cuffed, her heavy breasts peaked and flushed. The man teased her erect nipples until she begged aloud, crying out for him. He'd made love to her, eventually. It was what had gone before that Monica needed to know, right now. She had to see and feel the cuffs locking over those slender wrists. Urgently, and with her hands shaking, she reached inside her pocket and pulled out the cuffs. Clasping them in both hands, she lifted them above the bed, and saw it all.

"Strip," the man instructed after he'd finished spanking her, then quickly brought her to orgasm with his fingers on her clit and his thumb inside her tight anus. She was still on her hands and knees at that point, her entire body shuddering from the extent of her climax. Then she clambered to her feet and took off her clothes.

"Get on the bed," he'd instructed, "and show me that wet pussy of yours."

The woman did as instructed, feline in her grace, her eyes bright and shining from her orgasm, her face flushed. Glancing back at him while she climbed onto the bed on her hands and knees, she rolled onto her back, opening her legs. She was submissive but playful, and Monica sensed their understanding of each other's needs was fully formed. The woman's mischievous streak fired his need to dominate her—it was an alliance that was borne of a long-term relationship. Monica felt it in her soul and ached to have even a taste of something similar, but it couldn't be. Her peculiar gift in life was a burden when it came to actually having a relationship, because sometimes she experienced too much history and things she didn't want to know. That was how it had been with Harry, her ex, at any rate.

The man had undressed, and his cock was erect and ready to be inside his partner. Before he kicked his clothes to one side he pulled the cuffs out of his jacket pocket and clambered between her legs, showing her the gem-studded item.

The woman cooed and wriggled on the bed, offering her hands to him. He'd captured her wrists in one hand, locking them together. Then he moved them over her head and pinned them on the pillows as he probed inside her with his long, hard cock. Monica closed her eyes over the image, savoring it.

The woman cried out loudly, as if the bondage freed her somehow, and Monica's core ached, her pussy slick. She had to find release. With her free hand, she lifted her skirt and slipped one hand inside her underwear, quickly massaging her clit before the image faded entirely. It was the look of that woman being pleasured while she was rendered physically powerless by the cuffs that pushed Monica close to orgasm. When she came, it was with the cuffs clutched firmly in one hand, the other hand locked on her pussy.

As she recovered, she stared down at the bed and when she touched it again she saw that they had slept spooned together. Neither of them had even realized they'd scraped the headboard with the cuffs. It made her smile.

At her belt her phone vibrated, breaking her connection to the night before. Inhaling deeply, Monica grounded herself in the here and now, hastening her skirt back into place. With one finger under the phone she tipped it up and read the name on the screen. It was Arabella, the hotel director's secretary. She unclipped the phone and answered the call.

"Monica, can you come up to Flynn's office as soon as you can, there's someone he wants you to meet. A man. Two men, actually."

"Sure." Jesus, what timing. She'd been summoned to the director's office. That was unusual. She would have to freshen up before she went up there. "I'm right in the middle of collecting some lost property. Just let me make some quick notes before the suite is made over. I can be up there inside ten." She glanced over at the bathroom. "Any clue who they are?"

"None at all, but I think Flynn's going to ask you to take them on a tour of the hotel. Oh, and you better prepare yourself because they are both drop-dead gorgeous."

"Okay." Who could they be? Agents for a regular tour party booking, perhaps. That was the type of visitor Flynn occasionally asked her to take on a full hotel tour, although she usually got more notice than this. "I'll be right up."

Arabella chuckled as she hung up.

Reaching into her pocket, Monica pulled out a neatly folded handkerchief and dabbed the back of her neck, rueful of the interruption. Pocketing the handkerchief, she smoothed her hair and hurried into the bathroom, wondering all the while who the visitors were and why she had been summoned. It wasn't the best of times to have been indulging herself, but she hadn't been expecting anything like this to happen. She silently chastised herself for doing what she had done and being unprepared, especially if she had to show efficiency after what she'd just experienced. That was why it was a dangerous game to indulge in, and that was why she was wary about where and when she did it. When she had previously indulged, it was after hours. Today, she'd run with it too soon, on a whim.

"Shame you didn't think of that earlier," she told her flushed reflection in the bathroom mirror, annoyed.

Chapter Two

Interesting, Owen Clifford thought to himself.

Flynn Elwood, the managing director of Cumbernauld's of Kensington, was annoyed they had requested the housekeeping manager give them a tour of the place. Why was that?

Flynn Elwood shifted in his seat, his frown apparently welded to his forehead. "Mr. Clifford, I know you've come here with good intentions, but we have our own PR person. He's a good man and he deals with our in-house promotional developments."

"Of course you do, and rest assured I don't intend to step on his toes." Owen gestured magnanimously with his hands. "I know it isn't easy to have an outsider come in and try to give you advice about how to run things, but please accept it as a genuine offer of assistance from the Cumbernauld's Board of Directors. They only mean to help by offering suggestions for the good of the individual franchise as well as the entire chain, after all." Owen watched his host closely. *Look a gift horse in the mouth, buddy, and I'll start to wonder what you've got to hide.*

Flynn Elwood nodded, but didn't respond verbally. He was uncomfortable with the situation, Owen recognized that. Elwood was bound to be uncomfortable. He'd run this hotel franchise for fifteen years and now HQ had sent someone in to find new ways to increase the turnover. Well, that's why Elwood thought they were here.

Owen had come in under the guise of an ideas man which put a more positive spin on his actual role, which was to root out and expose the weak points. An agent provocateur of sorts—a henchman to some people's eyes—his job was never an easy one. He had to look for weak spots, dead wood, errors, theft and fraud, and find out who was at the back of it.

He then had to build up the hotel from that point, getting it back on track.

The profit margin at Cumbernauld's of Kensington had been diminishing over the last year, and his job was to find out why. *By any means necessary.*

Flynn nodded, awkwardly. "Of course, you're right. I was just surprised by your arrival. We would appreciate any input you have for us."

It was a forced acknowledgement. An expert in body language, Owen took in the awkwardness of Flynn Elwood's posture and the tension in his shoulders. Elwood averted his eyes and shifted papers about on his desk. The man was insecure.

"I want to continue our reputation as one of the finest London hotels," Flynn added. "This is a place where visitors can expect to sample the hospitality of a more sedate, traditional time in London. The hotel is synonymous with luxury."

"Absolutely. You offer something unique, even amongst the Cumbernauld's chain. That's what they are all about at HQ." Owen smiled. "I'd like to get to know the place better." He'd already done that. He'd stayed at the hotel as an anonymous guest a fortnight before and found nothing obvious. The hotel, staff and service seemed beyond reproach, from the outside. "And I'd like to meet the people who run it."

Elwood nodded. "I do wish you'd allow Sheila Trent, our chief accountant, to take you on the tour. She's been with me from the beginning of my tenure. She can give you an insight to the accounting side and show you the hotel."

"I'd like to meet her. Perhaps we'll do that tomorrow. I always like to go for grass roots to begin with. A member of the housekeeping staff is perfect for that." In his experience housekeeping staff were often the ones who heard and passed the rumors. They kept a watch on the staff at the top, noticing when they changed procedures. If someone was deliberately messing with the hotel's reputation—which was one possible scenario—the housekeeping staff would have heard about it.

Alec, his PA, signaled him from beyond Flynn's desk, catching Owen's eye. Alec had been studying the staff photographs, which were displayed in a large frame on the wall. He seemed to be trying to draw Owen over. Was it something about the housekeeping manager? A smile played around Alec's attractive mouth, instantly triggering Owen's curiosity. Owen knew Alec well enough to recognize that his interest had been captured by the photographs.

"Has the housekeeping manager been with you long?" Owen's attention was back with Flynn Elwood.

Elwood pursed his lips before answering. "Monica Evans is a good worker, she's been with us for over ten years, but you'll find her a bit of an ice queen."

That was some inappropriate comment. Owen's eyebrows lifted. This guy was really unsettled. He rose to his feet and was about to cross to the wall-mounted frame and take a look at this Monica Evans, when the door clicked open and he got to see the housekeeping manager in the flesh, instead.

As soon as he saw her, he knew he'd seen her before, when he'd been undercover. He recalled watching her as she glided through the hotel, the epitome of British reserve and efficiency. She'd always had a small, smart electronic notebook clipped to her waistband. How fortuitous that he'd attached himself to her, or maybe not. She was incredibly attractive. He couldn't afford to be distracted from the job. However, the job was supposed to be done by any means necessary. If he had to spend time with Monica Evans, maybe this project would be more pleasant than he had expected.

Elwood had called her an ice queen. He couldn't think of anything less appropriate. On the surface, perhaps. Pale blonde hair neatly clipped up, immaculate business suit and heels. Nothing in the least bit suggestive or raunchy in her demeanor or attire. If he went on presentation alone, he might be tempted to believe the ice queen moniker. But her face told an entirely different story. Flushed, wide-eyed and aroused, she seemed acutely aware of herself and everything around her. Her blue eyes were unnaturally bright and her soft lips were full and parted. Frankly, she looked as if she'd just had a hurried grope with the concierge in a broom cupboard.

"Flynn, you requested my presence?" Her gaze darted around the office, taking in the three of them, then settled on her boss as she awaited his instruction.

Owen decided to intervene. Why wait?

Flynn Elwood issued an introduction from behind the desk, explaining their presence, but Owen stepped between the hotel owner and the attractive blonde and put out his hand. "Monica Evans, pleased to meet you. I'm Owen Clifford."

The woman stared down at his hand as if it were on fire.

He reached in and grasped her hand. She shook it briskly then tried to pull free, eyeing him with an almost accusatory expression when he didn't allow her to do so.

Holding her small hand tightly inside his, he placed his free hand on her forearm, holding on to her and moving closer as he continued to speak. "I've come down here under instruction from Cumbernauld's Board of Directors. My remit is to make suggestions about hotel promotions and the like."

He gripped her hand tighter still as he spoke. His colleagues called his handshake his secret weapon and he always cashed in on that in his work, connecting with people on a personal level.

Again, she tried to pull free.

Again, he kept hold of her, and when he did, her façade faltered.

Her eyes widened, and her lips parted in the most sensuous way. She took a deep, audible and faltering breath, and her pupils dilated. "Owen Clifford," she repeated, somewhat breathlessly, her gaze shifting from his hand back to his face.

Oh, if only he could read her mind. But her body told him enough. The way she looked at him made his blood pump south. This one was aroused, and she looked at him as if it was his fault. Surprised, Owen grinned. "It's an absolute pleasure to meet you. I hope you don't mind if we attach ourselves to you?"

"Attach yourself?" Her question came out on another breathless rush and she seemed now to be savoring their connection, her eyelids lowering in a perfect gesture of submission, her hand softening within his grasp.

Even if his interest hadn't already been triggered, that would have done it. "Yes, my assistant and I will be here for a few days while we see if we can introduce some new ideas for promoting Cumbernauld's."

She glanced at Alec, and back at him, and for one strange moment he thought she might have sensed something about him and Alec, something about their out-of-office-hours relationship, but he shook it off. How could she know that they were lovers as well as business colleagues?

She swallowed hard before she responded. "I'll do what I can to help."

Her gaze met his again, and Owen had the feeling that she was not only shocked by him, she was aroused by him—and blatantly interested as a result. Whatever he had done to provoke that reaction, he sure as hell hoped he could do it again.

Chapter Three

Get a grip of yourself.

Monica was trembling. She led the way through the hotel while she delivered her standard talk about the facilities. It was a talk that was well rehearsed and delivered over and over, and yet her legs still felt weak under her. He hadn't wanted to let her hand go, and that meant his sexual aura swamped her. She was barely recovering from that when he introduced his assistant.

Apparently she had to spend time with them both, which was going to stretch her to full capacity if that handshake was anything to go by. They were both charming and affable—and inside her personal space. The fact that they were both attractive made it difficult to resist the temptation to acquire more knowledge about them than she had already been introduced to, and that had her agog with curiosity.

Alec, the PA, was whip-lean and ultra fit-looking in his designer suit, with spiked blond hair and intense green eyes. His role was clearly to observe. Owen was built larger and his fitted suit only emphasised the breadth of his shoulders and his muscled physique. When he moved he seemed to glide, despite his size. He was dark, with closely cropped black hair and brown eyes that sparkled with humor and intelligence. Alec was pin-up boy attractive, whereas Owen was more rugged. Both of them were exceptionally good looking in their own way, their smart tailored suits hinting heavily at their business caliber. There wasn't a woman on the planet who would be able to resist them.

Owen had held onto her hand for so long that she couldn't stop the heady and intimate knowledge of this attractive man entering her psyche. Not only was his sexual history thrust upon her, it was so vivid that it instantly fired her libido. Owen Clifford was a dominant, a sexual adventurer, and he sometimes played with men as well as women. When she had looked down at his hand she saw that hand on his assistant's shoulder. She saw it on his naked back and moving lower. *Too much.* She'd been about to demand he let go when he finally did.

When she was introduced to Alec Stroud he was easier for her to cope with, but his sexual energy was fierce, nonetheless. Could it be true? Were they both bisexual? If it hadn't been for her peculiar talent, she never would have guessed. And now she was fascinated. She shouldn't be, but she couldn't help it.

It was when they were on the second floor of the guest rooms that she got her chance to find out for sure. She was behind them while they looked into a standard guest room, and Alec went for his hip, pocketing the visitor's ID card he'd been issued. When his keys dropped out of his back pocket, Monica couldn't help herself. It was a split second decision, but she wanted to know. She dropped down and scooped them into her palm. They were warm from his pocket and as she straightened up, she opened herself to them quickly, before he had a chance to turn around and take them back.

She saw the two men on either side of a desk in an office. It was the end of the day and the place was quiet. Owen was seated, powerful and attractive as he considered the man on the other side of the desk—his lover, Alec. Alec was tense, waiting for instruction. Owen laid a key on the desk between them. Monica's hand closed over the keys in her palm. It was a key to his house, and Alec would go there later, with a woman. They both made love to her, and the morning after she'd gone they'd taken a shower together. An image of Alec with his face to the tiles—sudsy water running down his muscled back—flashed through her vision. Then the sounds of his pleasured moans echoed through her mind.

"Thanks."

Monica's head jerked up when she heard Alec's voice.

He lifted the key fob out of her palm and pocketed them, his expression curious. She smiled and tried to pull herself into shape. She felt like she'd had too much of a good thing today, overdosed. She'd only seen the briefest of images, but the relationship between them and what happened afterwards was far too ready to burst through. She tidied her collar and walked on down the corridor. When she knew they couldn't see her, she smiled. Now she knew for sure. They were lovers, and they shared women.

When they reached the service elevator, she pressed the button and tried not to stare at them. "The majority of the next floor is given over to the gym and spa facilities. We can grab coffee in the after-sports bar there, if that suits you both?"

"Sounds good," Owen confirmed as they entered the elevator.

It wasn't until the doors slid shut that she realized this was the first time the three of them had been entirely alone, and it was in a small, private space. The east end service elevator was the smallest of the range, only big enough for two housekeeping staff and one trolley. The mirrored walls only served to fill her vision with the two men who accompanied her. Her pulse responded to their proximity. She quickly pressed the button.

The lift moved then ground to a halt and juddered dramatically.

Monica's stomach knotted. "Not now," she murmured under her breath. *Please.*

"Problem?" Owen asked.

"This service lift has been troublesome these past couple of weeks." She'd made it a priority and had assumed it had been fixed. This was all she needed while she showed them around. A black point against her name, for sure, not to mention the fact she was now stuck in here with them. “It’s one of the older mechanisms in the building. We’re about to have it replaced, but it’s important that all features—even those predominantly used by staff—fit the old world specification of the hotel.”

She pressed the alarm button and flicked open her phone. To her dismay, maintenance had voicemail on. “Monica Evans here. The service lift has stalled again. I’m in it with two very important visitors from headquarters. Please get down here as soon as possible.

“They won’t be long,” she assured them as she disconnected, and hoped that would be the case. She forced a smile and wished that she could get a grip. *Too much input today. No one’s fault but my own.*

Owen rested his hands in his trouser pockets and shrugged his shoulders. “It’ll give us time to talk. Perhaps you can help me out.”

Oh great, he was pleased they were stuck in here. Her smile tightened. She would prefer it if they talked as they walked. Luck was against her on that score. She fiddled with the phone at her belt, then her electronic notepad, trying to distract herself from his looming presence and their close proximity in the limited space of the stalled lift. “You’re the ideas man. What is it that you want, Mr. Clifford?”

“Call me Owen, please. I’d like your company at dinner tonight, for starters.”

Her head jerked up. That was the last thing she’d been expecting him to say.

Both of them smiled her way, like two sleek alley cats eyeing their prey. She went hot and cold all over. Why did Owen Clifford stare at her that way? That handshake of his—the memory of it made her legs feel like jelly. The physical sensations it had let loose in her were unspeakably arousing, making her mind flit into dangerous territory, her body wired as desire built at her centre.

Then he moved away from the wall opposite and stepped closer, and she felt panic. If he touched her again while she was so aroused, she'd be swamped with sensation. He leaned against her side of the lift, and that put his chest right up against her shoulder.

Mustering herself she shot him a warning glance. "I'm happy to work with you while you are here, but I must ask you to respect my personal space."

Her pulse raced erratically. The palms of her hands itched to touch him and discover more. Her body was so keyed up that her psyche was reaching out for knowledge of him, of its own accord.

"Your personal space?" There was a faux innocence in his question that didn't match the devilish twinkle in his eyes.

God, he was insufferable. "Don't touch me." The warning was blurted out. "Please," she added, hoping for respect, pity, something.

However, he didn't step away. Instead he rested his elbow up against the wall beside her head, closing her in. "No touching?" He gave her a thwarted glance, making it obvious that he wanted to touch her, and more.

Monica glared at him, desire flaring ever higher inside her.

Curiosity filled his eyes. "Is this why they call you the ice queen?"

Her breath caught. *Ice queen?* How dare he? "Mr. Clifford, I don't know what you're doing here, but you are being rude and intrusive. It's clear to me that you're deliberately trying to unnerve me."

He smiled, as if he was pleased by that. "I can see you're an intelligent woman, and if we are going to be working closely for the next few days, after all, we need to be forthright."

The way he said closely insinuated that he wasn't going to respect her boundaries at all.

"There's forthright and there's downright rude." She laughed dismissively, trying to match up to him, when what she really wanted to do was something entirely different, something prohibited. An image of herself kneeling on the floor, begging for mercy, flitted through her mind, and she had to press her thighs together to stop herself staggering.

"I wasn't being rude. Someone else was." He paused deliberately, as if to let that sink in, and it did.

Someone else had called her that? Who?

"Maybe I didn't believe an attractive woman such as you deserved an inappropriate label like that."

Inappropriate? He could talk.

"Maybe I wanted to see your reaction." He scanned her face then her body with curiosity in those dark eyes of his.

So they did call her an ice queen. Monica was mortified.

On the one hand his revelation made her doubt the loyalty of her colleagues. On the other hand it was honest, exposing a working attitude she despised. Men snarking about women—bitter men, mostly. Yes, she'd turned a few of her colleagues down, Flynn Elwood included. Flynn was married, in fact his wife was the money behind his investment in the hotel, but that didn't stop him having affairs. She'd been one of his attempted conquests years back when they first worked together. It had been awkward between them for a while afterwards. Then they both ignored the fact that he'd made an improper suggestion and it was forgotten. Did that make her an ice queen in his eyes?

More to the point, why was it that Owen Clifford had stated it at all? To unsettle her, or to show her what was really being said? Then she studied him again, and his reassuring smile made her want to break free and run from everything she knew, because it made her want him, desperately.

"Even if it was said, you're obviously trying to upset me by repeating it," she said, with a serious note.

"No. I'm sorry if it appears that way. To improve the way things work here I need to find things out fast, and I find that in my line of work pulling the curtains wide open shows the dirt up pretty quickly."

That made sense, even if she didn't agree with his methods. What else had been said about her, she wondered. His motives were double-edged, and he made no effort to hide that. It didn't help that he was looking at her as if he wanted to undress her. "You're testing my loyalty, by revealing what they say about me behind my back?"

"Perhaps. Monica, the hotel performance isn't up to par."

Her eyes rounded, she couldn't help it. That statement seemed so wrong. "I find that hard to believe."

"Sorry, but that's why I'm here."

Could it be true?

He paused, watching her closely. "How loyal are you, Monica Evans? Got any dirt you want to pass back, now that you know what Elwood calls you?" There was no small amount of humor in his expression.

Jesus, he was provocative, and he'd moved even closer despite her warning. Alec, his assistant was amused too. She attempted to shift away, but she was in such a state she managed to do the opposite and gave him an excuse to touch her hip when she brushed against him.

"Oh, what have we here?"

His hand was against her jacket pocket and for one long moment Monica grappled with reality. What was it? Then she remembered—the cuffs. The jeweled handcuffs. Her eyes closed. *Shit.*

He pulled them out of her pocket, slowly, and held them up for his cohort to see. Light glinted off them and flashed around the mirrored walls.

"They aren't mine." She pressed her lips together, denying the urge to snatch them back.

"Not yours? Aww, I'm disappointed." His eyes flashed seductively. "I was hoping you'd give us a demo."

The flame of sexual interest that had faltered when he'd quizzed her too intimately flickered quickly back into life, her pussy aching in response to his words.

"The item is lost property. I have to log it." Her statement was almost vague, fascinated as she was by the way he looked holding the glamorous cuffs aloft, so powerful and so easily attuned to the suggestive object. "It's part of my job."

"But you kept them." He gave her a thoroughly wicked smile, his glance moving from the cuffs to her and back again.

It made her heart pump. "Actually, I was on my way to secure them when I was summoned to meet you."

He twisted them in his hand, looking at them with speculation. "I bet they made you curious."

She shrugged, secretly thrilled by the way the conversation was going, unable to resist following. "Maybe."

"Maybe? Don't even attempt to deny it, I can tell." He glanced her over, top to toe. "I can read your body language." His stare was both slow and deliberate. "And I'd put money on the fact you wanted to keep them."

He couldn't know that, she was sure of it. He was just guessing—taking a chance, had to be. But the very fact he took that chance fired through her, making a deep, intimate connection. He really was flirting with her, right in front of a man who she knew to be his sometimes lover and it set her alight.

She shook her head, trying to do it with nonchalance. "I can't keep them. But I can't help admiring objects like that if they pass through my hands. Is that so wrong?"

"No, not at all." He looked as if she had proven him right.

A shout came from above, and the lift jolted into action.

"Ah, the cavalry. Shame." He made the comment under his breath and with regret, tucking the cuffs back into her pocket, patting them in an almost fond and intimate manner. "You'll have dinner with us tonight, and when you do you can tell us why it is you don't like to be touched."

"You really have no shame," she murmured, deliciously shocked by his insistent attitude, despite the sure knowledge that she should resist the temptation of anyone getting that close to her secret.

What is wrong with me today? It was his fault.

His eyebrows lifted. "Personally I can't think of a single reason why you wouldn't want to be touched. You're the sort of woman who should be put on a pedestal, and adored. Don't you agree, Alec?"

Monica's heart raced. He'd finally drawn in his cohort. She glanced at Alec. He leant back against the mirrored wall of the lift, smiling a Cheshire cat smile. The silent, watchful observer. The right hand man. *His secret lover.*

"Absolutely, "he responded. "You should give it a try."

"Give a try," she repeated.

"Being put on a pedestal," he clarified, and his gaze covered her, speculatively.

She remembered the image of the woman they had shared when she held his keys. Her clothing felt tight and restrictive, her legs weak under her. The doors of the lift slid open, and there was a maintenance man in a boiler suit standing outside expectantly.

It was with some effort that Monica peeled herself away from the wall and stepped out into the corridor. With them both close behind her it was hard to be logical. She paused and thanked the maintenance man, trying to get a hold of herself. *Jesus, I don't even know what floor we're on.*

"You'll have dinner with us," Owen repeated, and he was so close against her that she felt his breath against the side of her cheek. His hand was a hair's breadth from her hip. It seemed to lure her with its heat, with its promise of pleasure.

Glancing back at him, she saw from his expression that it was an instruction, not an invitation. His eyes glinted with wicked humor, as well as essential male power. "Off the clock, okay?"

Off the clock? Monica didn't know exactly what he meant by that, but she didn't respond, because part of her loved that thrill—the thrill of not knowing. It was so rare, and so tempting.

Chapter Four

It was time to go down to the Byron Bar for the dinner date meet, but Monica was so strung out with nerves she couldn't leave her office. She wanted to go, she just wasn't sure it was the right thing to do. Reaching for the phone, she dialed her youngest sister, Faye.

"Hey Monica, you okay? You don't usually call at this time of day."

Monica gave a wry smile. All three Evans' sisters were psychic, and it was something they didn't share with anyone else. It also meant that they knew when they needed each other. "Just looking for some advice."

"There's a man, isn't there?" Faye was delighted.

It was all right for her, she had a better handle on her psychic ability. Being the youngest, she had witnessed her older sisters dealing with their psychic ability and had easily shrugged off many of the issues they had endured. As the youngest, Faye had never been alone with her strange ability the way Monica had, but somehow that meant she was able to support them both when things got difficult. They had always been there for her, and Faye was the bubbly, light-hearted one of the three. Besides, it was easier for Faye because her psychic ability was attuned to ghosts and the afterlife. From an early age she was able to communicate with the spirits of those who had passed on. It was when they were staying with their Aunt Agatha in her Victorian terraced house in Eastbourne one summer that they found out about Faye's gift. She kept chattering about what they thought was an imaginary friend, who actually transpired to be the ghost of one of the early inhabitants of the house.

"Yes, there is a man. Actually, there are two of them."

Faye laughed softly. "You want to know which one you should go out with."

"It's not quite simple as that." Monica tapped her fingers on the surface of her desk. "I can't explain it now, I haven't got much time. It's more about, you know, my secret. I'm worried that it will come out."

"You've let that put you off having a relationship for far too long. Take a risk, have some fun." Faye paused. "You know which one you are going to choose, don't you?" Again she chuckled. "Sounds like you've already made a decision to go out with him."

Faye was right. Except for one thing, she was going out with *both* of them. Curiosity had got the better of her and she wanted to know more about their relationship. She could always leave, if it got to be too much. She could claim it was inappropriate to socialize with fellow employees, if she felt too uncomfortable. Her body flared again as the images and sensations she had experienced in their presence flashed through her mind. That alone was a huge turn on. Then there was the fact that Owen Clifford was the most demanding, compelling man she'd ever met. "Yes I have decided. I'm nervous, I guess."

"Relax. Enjoy the date and let me know how it goes."

Monica was about to hang up, but there was something else she had to know. "Oh, I tried ringing Holly and her phone is off. I got an old feeling about it."

"Yes. Her phone is off because she's in hospital."

Monica sat bolt upright, her fingers clutching at the edge of the desk. "Is she okay?"

"Don't fret, she's fine. Her neighbor was involved in a car accident and she was first on the scene."

"How awful. Is the neighbor okay?"

"Yes, he's going to pull through but there was this one old thing…I wasn't going to say anything about as you have a date, but apparently she looked after this guy until the ambulance arrived. She called earlier and said that since it happened she's formed some sort of intense psychic link with him. Even while she was waiting in the corridor at the hospital, she could see and feel everything that was being done to him, you know, the tests and stuff."

Monica frowned. "Crikey, how weird is that?"

"I know!" Faye responded. Their middle sister, Holly, was the least psychic of them all. She was able to make future predictions and picked up on moods quickly, but unlike them she never had a specific talent. This was news indeed.

"I'll keep in touch with Holly," Faye assured her. "You go and enjoy your date and we'll talk tomorrow."

The chat had brought Monica back to earth with a thud, and she stood up and readied for the meet. It was a hospitality thing that was all. She mustn't read too much into it.

When she arrived at the Byron Bar, however, she saw Alec standing there on his own and with an expectant look on his face. She burned up with self-awareness. He had lost his tie and jacket and his shirt was open, giving her a look at his strong collarbone. There was a drink at his elbow and his eyes lit as she walked over to him.

He grasped her hand and drew it to his lips, kissing the back of it briefly. "Monica, what can I get you?"

That this was a date and not a work function was screamingly obvious. She pulled away quickly, but not quick enough—not before she felt hot lust pump from his skin to hers. "I'll have one of those."

He signaled the bar man. "Another G & T over here, please."

Jake, the barman, nodded at her as he reached for a glass. "Ms Evans."

She was glad she'd kept her suit on. It made it clear she was working, at least to the other staff. Nodding at Jake, she mustered him a smile.

When she glanced at Alec, he was watching her with an appreciative look in his eyes.

"So," she said, suddenly self-conscious under his close inspection, "how long have you been working for Mr. Clifford."

"He won't be happy if you keep calling him Mister."

She shrugged. "I was brought up well."

He smiled. "I can tell." He signed the bar tab before he continued. "I started working for Owen about two years ago. It soon grew into something far beyond a working relationship though."

Monica blinked. Had he really just put that out there?

"Over the last year we've become…well, inseparable, I suppose you could say."

Monica swayed, her legs growing weak under her. "Why are you telling me this?"

Alec watched her reactions closely. Everything about him was level and controlled. He was so sure of himself. "Because you are going to dine with us, and we believe in putting our cards on the table."

It was a characteristic she would normally admire, but the nature of what he had stated made her dizzy. The knowledge ran along her nerve endings, making her feel wired and edgy. She lifted her drink and sipped at it nervously.

Unfazed, Alec continued. "We discovered that we shared the same sexual interests, and we grew close."

She gave a disbelieving laugh. "That must have been some discovery."

"It was, and although we were attracted by each other's lifestyle it didn't come out for a while. It was quite tense there at the beginning."

He paused, and she felt as if he was acknowledging her state of nerves.

She put her glass back on the bar. "I can imagine."

"Once we discovered we were both bisexual, sharing our experiences with women proved to be the next logical—and fulfilling—step."

Monica could scarcely breathe, let alone form a response. Instead, she stared at the bottles on the shelves at the back of the bar while she gathered her thoughts. Alec was intent on filling in the gaps to enlighten her. The fact that she was already aware of their relationship didn't help. *And yet still I am here. I should leave now.* No doubt his words were made to put her at ease, but it actually meant it would be far harder for her to do a runner if she chose to, which made her all the more nervous.

"Why are you telling me this?" she managed to ask.

"Because you want to know."

"What makes you think that?"

"You're here, and you haven't done a u-turn yet." He grinned. His face was made for that grin. It made him even more attractive.

So, he'd taken a gamble in telling her. It felt like it was a test. She reached for her drink and this time she took a large swig and knocked it back.

"Come on," he added, "let's go upstairs."

Monica practically choked on her drink. "Upstairs? Isn't Mr. Clifford joining us?"

"No, we're joining him, in his suite."

"I thought we were having dinner…"

"We are. He's ordered a buffet."

The hand he put under her elbow didn't give her much option but to go with him, not without making a scene. It was the way they had taken over, redirecting the evening's events, that shocked her most of all. His confession was blatant, but she'd been pre-warned on that score. The shift to a suite was unexpected. She'd thought they would be in a public place. More or less immediately they were going to be alone again, and as she stepped into the lift with him she recalled what it had been like, being alone with them, earlier.

There was another couple in the lift and she stared across at them, rather than look at her companion's reflection. *What am I doing? I can't touch these men.* Nevertheless the lure was too great to resist. The chance to toy with the opportunity, to flirt with them awhile, that was too tempting. Too rare. *I'll step away if it gets dangerous.*

Alec held the door while the other couple got out, then lifted his hand and offered it to her. The gesture was compelling, and yet she knew she couldn't accept it. It pushed her to move, nonetheless. Gathering herself she stepped out of the elevator, resisting the hand. Alec stepped alongside her, leading her to the other end of the corridor where Owen's suite awaited. At the door, he paused and looked at her.

"Are you hungry?" His mouth moved in a sensuous smile.

It felt like a loaded question. The humor in his eyes got to her though, easing the tension she felt. She laughed, softly. "Let's just say my appetite has been kindled, but I'm not sure if I'll be able to eat any food."

He inclined his head in acknowledgement, then reached over and opened the door.

The suite was familiar to her, and she clocked the details as a matter of routine. It was a classic theme with wood panelling, wine colored carpet and brass highlights here and there. Rock music played through the sound system. It felt like a male arena.

Owen lazed in a chair by a table in the sitting room of the suite. What looked like buffet selection number three—one of the most interesting and delicious menus, all of which played on an aphrodisiac theme—was arranged on platters on the table nearby. That was laughable, none of them needed any help from aphrodisiacs, she was quite sure of that. The sexual energy off these two was zinging, and she felt permanently aroused around them. *So what the hell am I doing here?* The risks quickly stacked up, but they toppled from her mind when she saw Owen because he looked so damn good.

He sat with one leg dangling casually over the arm of the chair, and it appeared that his hair was still wet from a shower. The business suit was gone and he wore faded jeans and an open necked black shirt. His feet were bare. That seemed rather incongruous, as if it suggested something much more primitive and wild than the luxurious surroundings he currently inhabited.

As she approached he lifted something from one of the platters on the table and ate, slowly, all the while eying her up as if he'd rather be eating her. He resembled an emperor at leisure, and she was the sacrifice being led in by his right hand man. That should have scared her, and it did—but only in a way that aroused her. How could that be? This situation should have her running for the door. Yet there was an undeniable lure about Owen and Alec, as if they were the perfect combination of cocktail ingredients to tempt her.

Owen stood, and pulled out a chair for her, right next to his. She sat, trying to do so as nonchalantly as possible.

"Thank you." She wished her voice sounded more confident.

"My pleasure." Pulling his chair even closer to hers once she was in it, he sat facing her with an expectant smile on his face. He waited for her to say something.

Again, it felt like she was being given some kind of test. "So, have you had any good ideas yet?"

His smile grew and he lifted an eyebrow.

"Promotional ideas, for increased profit margins, I mean," she added quickly.

"One or two. But that's not what we are here to talk about, is it?"

"I thought you invited me to have dinner with you in the restaurant."

"I never mentioned the restaurant."

He was enjoying this, which was maddening because she felt thoroughly disarmed. They had a handle on this, she didn't. In the background she noticed that Alec poured champagne into flutes.

"We wanted to get to know you better. This seemed more appropriate."

The mischievous twinkle in his eyes made her wish she could be as easy in herself, as sure of what she wanted. But isn't that what appealed to her about him? She'd never met a man quite so sure of himself, quite so controlled and sexually aware. It was something she envied and admired. The scent of his cologne wafted over to her. She looked at his collarbone, revealed as it was in his open-neck shirt. His skin would be warm from the shower. She wondered what it would be like to feel that, to run her fingers over his bare chest. That would be dangerous with a man as sexually provocative as him. The energy he might radiate if she touched him that way would be full of personal and sexual images from his life, and her momentary encounter with Alec's keys made her even more cautious than she normally would be.

She accepted the flute of champagne and took a couple of sips, hoping it would steady her nerves.

"Tell us about Monica Evans." Owen reached for a lobster tail, dipped it in dressing and tore at it with teeth. He chewed it slowly while he considered her.

Monica took another sip from the glass and reached for the smallest canapé she could see on the table. Food was the last thing on her mind, but she needed the time to think.

"There isn't much to tell. My life revolves around my job and you already know all about that."

"No man, no family?"

She thought she was being clever with her response, but now she saw what he was getting at. He was checking the path was clear. They really were coming onto her. She knew that already, but she was still astonished by it. Normally she'd be keeping men at arm's length. Now she had two of them launching their seductive powers on her. What had gone wrong here? *You've walked into their world, and now you can't escape.*

The realization hit her and she swallowed hard. "No, no man. I live alone, if that's what you're getting at. I have two sisters, both younger than I am, and my parents are retired and live on the south coast."

"That sounds like a staff bio. I want to know about what makes Monica Evans tick."

Monica shrugged. She honestly didn't know what to say. There was more than the job, of course there was, there were two things in her life. Her job was the outer shell of her, the thing that kept the inner world under control. Her psychic self took up much of her energy and thoughts. It didn't leave much room for anything else, and she couldn't share it. The more he quizzed her, the more uncomfortable she felt about the fact she was hiding something. *I shouldn't have come.*

"Will you let us try to find out?" It was Alec who had said that, and she turned to look at him.

"Try to find out what?"

"What makes you tick."

He'd taken a seat slightly behind her, and he'd been observing the exchange all the while. When they made eye contact, he smiled and leant forward, resting his elbows on his knees. He had a more boyish charm about him than Owen, and he looked at her so adoringly that she knew he was the lesser predatory of the two. But they were predators, and she was in danger of falling completely under their seductive spell. *Can't do that. Too vulnerable.*

She put her glass back on the table, and as she did her hand shook. That was the last straw. "I think I should go. This was a mistake."

Rising to her feet she got up and walked away from the table as fast as she could.

Owen was at her back in a flash, his hands on her shoulders arresting her.

"Let me go." She braced herself, her hands fisting by her sides as she resisted touching him and obtaining psychic input. If she let his history with Alec in again, it would be too tempting to stay.

"You don't mean that." It was a statement, not a question, and he lowered his head alongside hers, breathing against the sensitive skin of her neck. His right hand was against her hipbone, easing her back against him. His left ran down her upper arm, soothing and arousing all at once.

She was helpless to resist. "Maybe not, but this is not appropriate."

"What isn't?"

"Fraternizing with work colleagues." Her prepared words came out stilted. Deep down she didn't want to use her excuse.

"We are all professionals, that won't change if we socialize outside of work hours. We are both discreet men. Besides, it might be disapproved of, but it's not actually a rule that is written and enforced. I know the company rulebook inside out, believe me. It's not unusual for people to meet through work. I could give you stats. I'm very good with stats…" He brushed one finger down the curve of her waist and around her hip. The subtle yet suggestive touch clung to her like static, crackling along her nerve endings. "You know," he continued, "how many workers have had affairs with their colleagues, how many enjoyed it."

Affairs. Monica cursed under her breath, her cheeks flaming. “You don’t believe in beating about the bush, do you?”

He turned her around and tipped her chin up in order to look deep into her eyes. How easily he controlled her when she had every intention of leaving.

“No. Life is too short…and you are exquisite. I want to watch you while you come. I want to be inside you when you do.”

“Bloody hell.” She glanced away, unable to meet his gaze, and yet she was completely unable to free herself from his magnetic draw, even though he only latched her to him with one finger beneath her jaw. It was then she saw that Alec had moved. He stood nearby and when they made eye contact he strolled over and joined them.

“Owen has a tendency to be direct.” He closed in on her back.

“So I noticed.” She felt Alec move behind her, and he kissed the back of her neck. When she reacted, lifting her chin, Owen smiled.

“It’s not often that attraction sparks between three people as quickly as it did with us,” he stated. “Surely you agree?”

It was the truth. Reluctantly, she nodded.

“You’re hiding something, that’s the only problem here.”

Panic swamped her. “It’s not what you think.”

“Tell me what it is and then there’s no reason not to stay and enjoy the company.” There was such a seductive invitation in his eyes and the husky tone of his voice as he whispered to her.

She swallowed. “I can’t. It’s personal.”

He continued to stare at her, and it was as if he was reaching down into her soul. “Is it about not being touched?”

"Are you psychic?" A sense of hope flitted through her. Was that what it was about him? The wisp of hope was soon quashed.

"No, just observant." His eyes narrowed, and he clasped her wrists inside his large strong hands, lifting them up above her head. "How does that feel?"

Stunned, Monica opened her mouth to object, but couldn't. The containment was too good. The way he took charge and controlled her physically that way shocked her to the core. Heady, delicious arousal sped through her. Her eyes flashed shut. A muted moan escaped her open lips.

"It feels good," Owen answered for her.

It did feel good. There was no point in denying it. Her reaction had given away just how turned on she was by his sudden maneuver. Shifting her weight from one foot to the other she squirmed in his grasp. The pounding between her thighs had taken her over. The fabric of her underwear clung to the damp heat of her pussy, and when her thighs rubbed against each other, it only made her situation worse.

When she opened her eyes he lowered her arms, but kept hold of her wrists. That curtailed her ability to touch him. It was the strangest thing. He had done it instinctively it seemed. She nodded, unable to form a reply. For a moment she thought he was going to let her go. Instead, he drew her closer still and kissed her.

When Owen's mouth covered hers, she offered no resistance. Desire swamped her and freed her of her secret—if only for a moment—she was all wanting. His tongue teased seductively along her lower lip. Her mouth opened. She heard her own startled moan under relinquishment in it. She couldn't help herself, she opened her mouth wider and teased her tongue along his. Meanwhile, Alec kissed her neck, his hands cupping her breasts from behind.

It was good that there was one of them on either side of her, because her legs became suddenly weak and her heels felt ridiculously unstable. The brush of Alec's thumbs over her erect nipples through her clothing made her moan again. Alec moved on it, unbuttoning her blouse and teasing his fingers along the exposed tops of her breasts while he kissed and licked the sensitive skin behind her earlobe. That sent a violent physical shiver through her.

Owen broke with the kiss. His eyes gleamed wickedly, making him look even more devilishly handsome. Alec stroked her from breast to hip, outlining her curves. The twin nature of their assault flooded her eager senses. They were playing her, and between them they were making her crazy. It had been too long, and this was too delicious.

Owen still had her wrists clasped in one hand, and he looked down at them. "Do you still have the handcuffs?"

The cuffs. Of course—that was why he'd done it, she realized. He thought bondage was something that she did, something that she knew. As she realized his intention it took the remaining strength from her knees. She swayed slightly, and Alec moved closer still, so that his body was against hers from the back of the shoulders to the backs of her calves. The hard length of his erection pressed against the small of her back through their clothing.

"I told you, they aren't mine."

"I don't care who owns them," Owen responded and his eyes gleamed with humor. "Do you still have them?"

Anxiety and arousal were assailing her in equal measures. He looked like a man driven, and the suggestion in his eyes sent her senses reeling. She shook her head. The handcuffs were locked in her drawer back in the office.

Alec was still tightly pressed against her back, and he nudged her ear with his nose then whispered to her. "We can improvise, if tying you up would make it easier for you."

That made her dizzy. She barely knew these men, but what she did know was that it was the inability to touch, the relinquishment of power to them, that enabled her to enjoy this crazy moment. Besides, the idea of them tying her up and seducing her was making her insane with lust. Closing her eyes, she let her head fall back against Alec's shoulder.

Alec chuckled softly and squeezed her hips tightly in his hands.

Owen bent to kiss her in the dip of her cleavage. Her head rolled. Alec moved his hands and slowly pulled her skirt up the length of her thighs. Each slow tug of the fabric revealed more than her thighs—she felt stripped bare by his actions. The way they took control made her pulse race and the damp heat between her thighs became sweltering.

She could have stopped Alec then, but she didn't.

And then Owen glanced down at her stocking tops with an appreciative glance. He put his hand between her thighs and cupped her pussy through the sheer fabric of her G-string. Direct and demanding, the touch of his hand on her pussy triggered a heightened need for release.

He stared into her eyes and one corner of his mouth lifted in appreciation. But the gentle squeeze he gave her there at her pussy made her gasp aloud.

"Oh, yes, you're ready for this. You want this every bit as much as we do."

We. The word echoed around her mind. Two of them. Could she really do this? She didn't have time to think about it because Owen nodded at Alec, and some silent agreement passed between them. Alec grasped her torso, and Owen ducked down and swept her feet from under her, his arms under her bottom and knees.

"Do you always manhandle women this way?" It was a feeble effort to maintain her cool façade, the one that was fast becoming a sham.

"Only beautiful blondes who secretly carry handcuffs on their person." Owen chuckled darkly as they carried her easily into the adjoining bedroom, where they deposited her on the bed.

It was a massive affair, easily big enough for three or more. Covered in a luxurious black satin quilt, it felt silky and cool beneath her body. It would be warmed through soon enough if things kept heading in the same direction. She was already on fire, and when she watched Alec pull his shirt over his head and abandon it, the temperature went even higher. His body was hard and fit, honed like an athlete. His fitness and stamina levels were unquestionable. The guy looked like he could go all night. And he was fast, because he was back beside her and taking off her shirt and bra, his nimble fingers quick with buttons and hooks. The proximity of his fit physique almost distracted her from what he was doing.

Meanwhile Owen stood at the end of the bed, watching while Alec undressed her. Then he lifted one of her feet, exploring the glossy patent leather of her high heel, before he slipped her foot free of it. His large hands clasped her ankle, then he reached up and stroked his hand over the surface of her stockings, an action which left her like a breathless rag doll under their twin assault.

"Beautiful," Owen commented when he ran his finger around the lace tops of her hold-up stockings, then he put two fingers beneath the lace, and stripped the stocking the length of her leg. When it was off, he tossed it to Alec.

Before she knew what was happening, Alec had used the stocking to bind her wrists together. When Owen stripped the second stocking off, he repeated the action and Alec used it to secure her wrists to the lavish headboard.

So that's what he meant about improvisation.

"Comfortable?" Owen asked, with no small degree of humor. He was amused by her need for bondage, as if it was a kink of hers. Little did he know.

Monica squirmed, and the tension in her arms and wrists felt deliciously decadent. Crazy though it was in her current state of arousal, she had never been so liberated in her life, because her number one enemy—her hands—had been locked out of this scenario. As she wriggled against the surface of the bed her breasts squeezed together and the nipples jutted out, hard and dark. Owen was staring at them.

Alec moved his attentions to her skirt. Unzipping it, he pulled it down the length of her legs. The only thing she now wore was her G-string, and when she glanced down she saw a tell-tale damp smudge on the front of the fabric. Pressing her lips together tightly, she moaned softly.

Alec trailed his fingers over her bare abdomen, which made her shiver. Meanwhile Owen stood at the end of the bed with his arms folded across his chest, his eyebrows lowered, and his expression thoughtful. When she glanced lower—and she couldn't help herself—she saw the bulge of his erection beneath the zipper on his jeans and her eyes flashed closed.

Alec ran his fingers beneath the band of her G-string then slowly pulled it down the length of her thighs. She wriggled her bottom and lifted it to assist. When she was entirely naked, she squeezed her thighs together, suddenly aware that Owen was still fully dressed, and Alec had only removed his shirt. She was naked. That, combined with her arousal, did strange things to her. She wanted to flee.

"Open her legs," Owen instructed.

The way he said it made her shudder. It was as if he knew she would find it hard, and Alec worked his magic instead.

First he inserted one finger between her thighs and stroked it up and down over the soft, sensitive skin there. Monica began to pant, her hips rolling against the bed covers. Still he stroked her. When the muscles in her thighs began to relax, he moved them apart. Then he lifted her feet wide apart at the ankle, exposing her pussy to Owen's watchful eyes.

The sound of her blood rushing thundered in her ears. For several long moments that and the music from the room beyond were the only sounds in the room. The two men remained in silence at her feet, while she was so thoroughly debauched and displayed. It was wildly arousing. She could barely stand to look at them, but she had to know what they were doing and what they were thinking.

When she glanced their way, she found Owen darkly brooding. Alec smiled, but she noticed he looked to Owen, as if waiting for instruction. It was obvious who held all the power here. Owen nodded.

Alec moved on the silent instruction. The bond between them had to be deep she realized, because he knew what to do. He climbed between her legs, moving towards her on his hands and knees.

"I'm going to prepare you now," he whispered, "then Owen will fuck you."

The statement left her speechless, but she didn't need to respond because he immediately ducked down and dipped his tongue into the damp groove of her pussy, easing back and forth over her swollen, sensitive clit.

The rush, the relief, the pleasure—for a moment Monica couldn't catch her breath. Then the lap of his tongue forced her to pant aloud.

With the fingers of one hand, he splayed open her folds, which made the contact more intense. Those fingers remained in place and rocked back and forth on either side of her clit, which made her core spasm and her hips roll, her body eager for more of his medicine.

Alec's cologne and the scent of his body reached her. His hands were now wrapped around her buttocks as he moved his tongue up and down the length of her pussy. The muscles in his shoulders rippled. All the while she could see Owen watching from beyond. Watching as his lover performed cunnilingus on the woman he intended to fuck. Her breasts lifted, the nipples needling with sensation. Her clit felt unbearably tight and hot, but Alec's rapid tongue movements were pushing her ever closer.

Owen's eyes were so dark they were almost black, and when she made eye contact, he unbuttoned his shirt and dropped it, then moved his hand over his erection. The action was like a promise. His smile had now become tight, his pent-up lust evident in his posture. It was almost as if he was jealous that Alec was there, but that did it for him—she could see it there in his expression. Even though he was controlled, he was barely holding back. He actually looked as if he was about to reach in and pull Alec off her. The thought of him coming at her with all that lust building, and soon, made her lips part with anticipation.

Then Alec sucked hard on her clit and thrust a finger into her sex, and she hit her peak. The sudden rush of release made her arch and twist in the bindings that held her wrists.

By the time she surfaced from the orgasm, Owen had stripped off his jeans and was rolling a condom onto an impressively long and hard erection. Alec had shifted, making way for him. He'd moved to the side of the bed, where he stood up and quickly unzipped his fly. When his cock bounced free, he wrapped his fist around the shaft and began to ride it up and down.

Christ, she realized, he was going to stand there and watch, while he masturbated. It was so horny and so beyond anything she had ever experienced, that she pressed her head back into the pillows and stared at the ceiling for a moment to assure herself it was really happening.

Then Owen was between her legs. He kissed her below her naval, drawing her attention back.

"My turn." He shifted and pushed his tongue into her sex, an action that made her feet lift from the bed.

She was still experiencing the aftermath of her first orgasm and the firm thrust of his tongue into her hole meant she was back there inside a heartbeat.

"Oh yes, you taste good."

It was almost a relief when he withdrew his tongue. He licked her clit once, twice, three times, and each time her body jerked against the bedcovers, so sensitive was she from the last round. Then he climbed over her.

Resting on his elbows, he stared down at her, locking her gaze with his. Then he eased his cock inside, stretching her open and filling her.

The garbled cry of relief she gave was a sound she barely recognized as her own voice. Sheer bliss rolled over her. Her centre throbbed wildly when the blunt head of his cock pressed deeper, then he drew back and thrust again. Panting for breath, she felt consumed by him, and when he put his hands beneath her buttocks and lifted her, manipulating her physically while he thrust in and out of her, a second orgasm built to fever pitch.

He nudged her thighs, encouraging her to wrap her legs round his hips. When she did so, his cock bowed inside her and stroked the front wall of her sex.

"Oh, oh," she moaned.

"Yes, right there, huh?" He began to thrust faster, massaging her right there in that sweet spot.

His forehead gleamed, the depth and rhythm he maintained pushing her closer. She could hear the sounds of their bodies, the slippery, slick pull of her wet pussy as he worked his cock into her. When her head rolled she saw that Alec was fisting his cock faster and faster, his free hand locked around his balls. The head of his cock was dark and swollen, the slit oozing. The arm that pumped his shaft was roped with muscle.

Her entire groin was aflame. She was close, so close to coming that her back arched and her fingernails bit into her palms. Then she caught sight of Alec coming. The fist that had been locked around his balls moved, and he filled it with his semen. Deep in her core she spasmed in direct response to that sight, her groin flooding with sensation.

Owen cursed under his breath and thrust ever harder.

All that pent-up energy she'd seen in Owen was being worked out now. His hips moved like a well-oiled machine, pumping hard and fast. The muscles in his neck and shoulders were tight, his pupils dilated as he watched her and forbade her to look away as he probed her deepest places.

"Owen," she managed to whisper, when she began to flood again.

He nodded. "Oh yes, I can feel you." He paused as if to savor what her body was doing. He shook his head then thrust again, he kept his cock right there, grinding his hips against hers as she came.

The release was so great that she hung limp in her bindings, but the hard rod of his cock inside her and the pressure of his body against her clit kept her there. A second wave washed over her, her thighs shuddering against his hips as her every nerve ending was strung out with the raw pleasure of another heady orgasm.

"Owen," she whispered again, and this time it was with gratitude.

"I knew you were no ice queen," he said from between gritted teeth, then his cock jerked and his head lifted, his eyelids lowering as it jerked again, his body taut and arched as he pumped himself into her.

Chapter Five

Owen awoke to the sound of the shower running. A quick glance at the clock told him that it was Alec in the bathroom. His partner was always up and busy before six. Alec was wired that way because he needed little sleep.

When he glanced back, he smiled. Monica was still there, asleep in his bed. Her sleek blonde hair was loose on the pillows, her adorable lips slightly parted as she dozed. He thought she might have taken off in the night. When she'd arrived she was as a nervy as an untamed bird, wary of the cage and yet tempted by it. At other times she seemed supremely calm to the point where he could understand the label they'd given her. It did not suit the woman they'd made love to last night, however. There were two sides to Monica Evans, and he wanted to know them both, intimately.

He allowed himself the pleasure of admiring her naked form. At some point in the night she had unraveled the stockings and she now had them clutched between her hands. She had allowed them to untie her from the bed, but requested they leave her wrists bound together.

"It makes me feels safe," she had whispered from under lowered eyelids.

"You really are into bondage," Alec had commented.

"I am now." She had lifted her eyelids and stared at Owen in a way that made him want to keep tied up forever. Willing she was, no doubt about that. Yet she seemed somehow disarmed by the bondage. She also seemed innocent of the intense draw she had on him. He was already feeling possessive about her. That was unusual, and he struggled to come to terms with it.

She'd snuggled close against his shoulder. Alec had brought several of the food platters over to the bed and they took turns feeding her. She was a strange one though. She seemed most comfortable when discussing the hotel. That was not really a problem, because they were here to learn about it and discover the weak point. But she seemed devoted to the place. She described the design of the other suites and told them some anecdotes from when the place was refurbished. She even talked about the buffet menus as if she'd been the chef who designed them.

Surely her job couldn't be her whole world, Owen wondered as he watched her sleeping. She was far too beautiful and far too sensuous to have that be the truth.

Just then she rolled over in her sleep and clutched the stockings tighter. It made her look adorably cute, as if she held a comforter. Her position also meant her breasts were squeezed gently together. Her nipples were tilted up and he had to resist the urge to lean in and run his tongue over them. His cock grew hard as he thought about it. She might like to be woken up that way. It was too soon for him to know, but he would endeavor to find out soon enough.

The arch of her waist and the curve of the hip made him long to stroke her. The sheet covered her from the hip down. When he looked back to her face her breathing altered, and her eyelids fluttered open.

Owen reached over and stroked the soft, warm, womanly curve of her abdomen. That made her smile.

"Good morning," she said, and her cheeks flushed as she looked around the room and realized she was still naked on his bed.

He now had a full on erection. Ducking his head, he kissed her gently, brushing his lips over hers. When he drew back, he pulled the stockings from between her hands and dropped them on the bed. He went to stroke the palm of her hand, but when he did she snatched it away.

She bolted upright as if she'd been physically slapped, turning around and putting her feet quickly to the floor.

His thoughts focused, fast. *The personal space thing, of course*. When she'd been bound she'd acted differently, as if she didn't mind the contact. He'd assumed they'd pushed her past it, but now he wondered if it was the bondage itself that had forced her through it. Curious, he reached out and rested his hand on her shoulder.

She moved, gently shrugging it off.

"You're a fascinating woman, Monica."

She glanced over her shoulder. "Why, 'cos I'm freaky about being touched?"

Something akin to resentment flared in those astute eyes of hers.

"That's just one of many reasons."

There was sadness in the set of her mouth, and it made him hanker to understand her. It also made him want to kiss her again.

She stood up and scouted around as if looking for her clothing. Then she was getting dressed, super fast, as if readying herself to leave. Owen frowned. It was scarcely six. Once Alec was done with his shower he would order breakfast. He wanted her to stay. They could enjoy the meal together, and plan another rendezvous. For some reason he couldn't bear the idea of her leaving, in case it was a one-off. Something about this woman had captured his attention, and he was pretty sure Alec wanted more too.

"You don't have to go yet."

"I do. I shouldn't have done this." She shot him a regretful glance.

As she dressed her lips remained tightly shut. She really believed it was wrong, even though she wanted it. Owen wondered if she really didn't do this kind of thing. That would explain a few of her responses. He wondered too if she'd ever had a multiple orgasm before. Something had made her stay the night before. Perhaps it was the bondage. Maybe she needed to be submissive. Perhaps having two guys did it for her and she hadn't had that kind of opportunity very often before. Whatever it was, she wanted more. He could see it in the sidelong glances she gave him as she dressed, but she was still as wary as a bird about to take its first flight.

The sound of the shower had stopped.

She shoved her feet into her shoes and glanced at the bathroom. "I better go."

Owen's attention sharpened. She wanted to be gone before Alec appeared. Couldn't trust herself to leave if they were both there. It was imperative he make her stay. He was on his feet a split second later.

"I don't want you to go." He grasped her shoulder, forced her to face him.

"Please, I have to." She struggled and wrenched free.

"Jesus, Owen." Alec stood there with his hands on his hips, watching. He had a towel around his waist and his hair and chest were both dripping wet from the shower. The look in his eyes was warning enough.

Owen was taken aback. Had he been too forceful? He walked the line, he knew that.

Monica took her chance and was at the door inside a heartbeat.

Owen strode after her. "We still have to work together."

He tried hard to make that sound like a simple statement of fact, rather than a threat. He didn't want to get heavy-handed, but it came out sounding much more demanding than he meant it too.

Slowly, she lifted her gaze to meet his. "I know."

There was desire in her eyes, and perhaps a plea for understanding.

Taking a risk he reached out to cup her cheek. Her lips parted, her eyelids lowering, and she moved her face within the cup of his palm. *She did like to be touched.*

"I'm sorry if I came across as insensitive." He stroked her cheek with his thumb, building on the tentative consent she exhibited now.

"You've been patient with me, thank you," she responded. She was studying him, weighing him up. Alec wandered over and joined them. She glanced from one to the other of them and sighed. "Give me some time, it's hard for me. I promise you it's not what you think."

Owen lifted an eyebrow. "What do I think it is?"

"Most people think that I've been abused or harmed in some way. It's not that, I assure you. It's something that makes me feel vulnerable, something I've kept secret for a long time."

Owen's curiosity was raging, but he didn't want her to feel vulnerable. What he wanted was the exquisite willingness they'd witnessed last night, the joy she took in her submission and the pleasure she gained from the experience. It was hard to reel in the urge to pressure her, but he knew he had to try, or she would walk out that door and never return.

Removing his hand, he nodded. He didn't know quite how patient he could be, but he would give her some space if that was what she wanted, because he could tell she would come back for more if he did so.

Alec shifted, resting one elbow on the door beside her. "We're good listeners."

She smiled. "I know." She glanced from one to the other of them. "I had a great time last night, thank you."

"Can we do it again?" Owen couldn't hold back. When Alec threw him another warning glance, he shrugged. "I'm a pushy guy when I want something, so shoot me."

"I like that about you," she commented.

Owen felt sure it was significant. Did men only get close to her if they were pushy?

She straightened up. “You assured me that we would be able to remain professional, that you would both be discreet. Does that still stand?”

“On all fronts,” he replied.

She reached for the organizer that she kept clipped to the waistband of her skirt. “I have to supervise my staff this morning. I suggest we meet in-house at the Shelley’s Corner House Pub for lunch, and we can resume our official business then. Does one o’clock suit you both?”

Alec smiled. “Anything else can be cancelled, right Owen?”

“Too bloody true.”

“Good.” She made a note on her organizer and replaced it at her belt. “In that case I’ll see you then. Have a good morning.”

After she’d shut the door behind her, Owen shook his head. “The consummate professional. It’s like a mask she slides into place.”

“That’s it exactly.”

Owen looked at his partner and he could tell that Alec was as intrigued by her as he was.

“Do you think that she knew that we’re lovers, when she first met us?” Alec asked.

Owen nodded. “She knew.”

“I mentioned that we were both bi when I brought her up here last night, but some of the women we’ve been with just don’t think about what that means, they think it’s all about them.”

“Monica understands the implications.” Owen was sure of it. Something in her eyes assured him of that. That was part of what appealed to him about her. “Any idea what her secret is?”

Alec gave him a disbelieving stare. “What do you think I am, psychic?”

* * * *

Sheila Trent, the head accountant for the hotel, seemed delighted when Alec turned up in her office—or that's the impression she gave. Monica had been wary, which was to be expected, but this woman was all about showing off her wonderful accounting system.

Sheila Trent beamed at Alec. She was a mature woman with a blatant, forthright manner—to the point of being pushy. The look she chose was designer clothing, eccentric earrings, and low cut tops. Her hair was dyed auburn and immaculately styled in a classic bob. In short, she was a smart, attractive and efficient-looking older woman who may or may not be a cougar. He never would have guessed she was an accountant.

"Take a seat," Sheila encouraged, pulling a chair close alongside her own. She patted it invitingly as she gave him a deliberate and approving once over.

As Alec sat down he found himself engulfed in a heavy floral scent. She launched into her introduction to the accounting system, flashing through pages at a rate of knots. Even though he listened closely and assessed the system for security while she described it, Alec couldn't stop himself glancing at his watch occasionally, counting the hours until their lunch date with Monica.

"Weren't there supposed to be two of you?" Sheila asked, at one point.

"My colleague was called away on an important matter."

Owen had gone to buy some toys for Monica, bondage toys. They had discussed and agreed it wouldn't take two of them to look into the accounts set up. Owen had plans to introduce himself to the restaurant management staff later that day. However, Alec's growing concern was that Owen was losing sight of his goal, because he was focusing somewhere else instead. In fact they were both in danger of falling into that trap. It was something he was going keep an eye on, and mention, if necessary.

"As you can see," Sheila informed him as she scrolled through the database, "we've made some minor adjustments to the system recommended by headquarters. Improvements, in my opinion." She gave him a smug smirk.

Alec tried not to react too obviously to that statement, which immediately had his attention. With a nod of encouragement, he asked her to continue. On she went. Would the changes they had instigated allow for things to fall through the cracks? The only way to tell would be to spend some serious hours going through the system. The easiest way to do that would be to bring in a USB drive and copy the database, get it onto his laptop, and take it apart. It was just the sort of thing he liked to get his teeth into.

"Can you run a simple purchasing order through the system so that I can see it working? It's a standard check we're asked to do. A box I have to tick." He gave her as most charming smile.

"Yes, of course. Let me take you next door and introduce my assistant. She deals with all the purchasing orders."

Alec noticed that she seemed pleased that he was moving on. He definitely wanted to have a look into those 'minor adjustments to the system' of hers.

Sheila's assistant turned out to be a woman in her mid-thirties with a pensive expression.

"This is Miss Mooney. Jane, can you run a purchasing entry through to show Mr. Stroud the system in action?" When the assistant nodded, Sheila Trent went to take her leave. "Anything else you need while you are in the accounts department, just ask Miss Mooney."

One thing was for sure, he had successfully convinced her that this was a perfunctory visit. Alec smiled at

Miss Mooney and hoped she was a little more accessible. The woman gave an unwilling half-smile and a nod in his direction. Alec quickly nicknamed her Miss Moody. He figured it was fair game, seeing as someone here had wrongfully nicknamed Monica the ice queen. She wore her hair scraped back in a ponytail. Unusually, she was dressed in what looked like professional cycle gear. It was either a fashion statement or she was one of the army of London cycle commuters.

Pulling up a chair, he sat down to study the procedure, but not without a quick glance at his watch. Three hours until lunch with Monica. Would they find out more about her then? He hoped so. She had them both fascinated.

Could she trust them? Monica sat at the desk in her office staring at her computer monitor with unseeing eyes. Thankfully the morning of regular duties had leveled her head and she'd been able to grab a few private moments before she met them for lunch. All morning she had been thinking it through, from the moment she stood under the shower in the staff changing rooms and let the warm water soothe her troubled thoughts. She'd come to the conclusion that if she wanted to continue the liaison, she was going to have to trust them with her secret—and she did want to continue the liaison. They were both attractive and attentive, and the opportunity to enjoy herself for a short time was too good to turn down. Even the night before, while they had chatted and grazed on the aphrodisiac buffet, she'd felt the wild urge to throw caution to the wind and explain why touching was difficult for her. It had been hard to hold back on the urge, but that line of behavior was deeply engrained.

The exchange they'd had that morning had forced her to face up to the fact that it was going to come out. If it did, she had to be in control of how. She arranged the lunch meet because she vowed to decide one way or the other in between. It was the practical thing to do. Either she put an end to it now and protected her secret, or she confided in them. There were risks on either side. They might laugh in her face if she confessed, or dismiss her as a freak. They didn't seem that brash or inconsiderate though.

If she didn't end it now it would have to end at some point, she knew that, but the night before had been astonishing. She'd been able to let go and enjoy sex completely, for the first time ever. It was because they hadn't let her touch them. Bound and helpless under the power of their joint seduction, there was nothing she could do but enjoy.

Briefly, her sensitive hands had no longer been her number one enemy. Was it luck? Because she'd had those diamante handcuffs on her person—had he assumed that she was into it because of that. Or was it them, something they always did when they seduced women? Monica didn't know, but she wanted to find out. She wanted more of what she'd tasted.

However, it was dangerous and she could be hurt. She could be compromised about her job as well, and that alone should make her cautious. Her job was her lynchpin. She needed the order Cumbernauld's brought into her world to cope with the less ordered part inflicted on her by her psychic ability. But when she tried to leave them that morning and saw them both standing there looking so goddamned gorgeous, she knew she would regret it for the rest of her life if she didn't let herself have this moment, for as long as it lasted. It wouldn't last long, she knew that. Attractive men like that, they would move on. This was a convenient thing for them because they were here and she doubled up as a confidante and a lover. Then she thought herself in that category—the easy lay—and it stimulated an inevitable ache in her chest, a longing for something that she would never be able to have, a proper relationship. But she wasn't going to deny herself the physical pleasure that she'd been offered via this liaison.

She was jolted away from her reflections when her desk phone rang. It was Flynn. "Good morning, Flynn. What can I do for you?"

"I wanted to apologize for sticking those two suits on you."

"Don't worry about it. It's all part of the job." Monica covered her eyes with her hand. What a sham.

"There wasn't anything I could do about it. I wanted to put them with Sheila, who would have been much more appropriate, but they insisted on the housekeeping manager."

It flashed through her mind that she could easily have missed out. That made her want to cling on to the chance she'd been offered and enjoy the moment.

"Like I said, no worries." She hated to lie, but she had to say something. "I treated it like a regular agent tour duty." She had done, up to a point.

"I'll try to convince them to move on with someone else, you're busy enough as it is."

She pressed her lips together. *No, I don't want that.*

"In the meantime, I want you to let me know what they ask you about."

She slumped onto her elbows. "They haven't said a lot about their…end of things."

She rolled her eyes. The conversation was farcical. If he didn't hang up soon she'd end up laughing down the phone.

Flynn, however, seemed determined to quiz her. "What *did* they ask you?"

She nibbled on her lower lip then resorted to turning the tables. "Are you worried about something in particular, Flynn?"

Silence.

"I mean, is there anything you'd like me to be aware of?"

Flipping it on him had done the trick. Eventually he replied. "I just want the place to come off looking good in front of the Board."

"It will. Cumbernauld's is the best. They are only here to see what could be improved. They might not come up with anything, but I'll keep you in touch with any comments they make…about the running of the hotel."

Mercifully, he hung up soon after and Monica slumped back in her chair. As ludicrous as the conversation had been, it had stripped her of some of the tension she felt, which was a good thing. Her boss's concerns were elsewhere, which made her feel as if hers should be too, but she was sure Cumbernauld's couldn't be improved upon, so that balanced it—kind of. She smiled to herself. All the chat had done was make her want to see them again, and be glad of the chance. When she stood up to go she still wasn't sure if confiding in them was the right thing to do, but she was ready to take the next step.

She arrived at Shelley's Corner a few minutes early to select a comfortable banquette in a quiet area. The two men walked in together a minute later. Alec was in the lead, like some kind of scout. She noticed how vibrant he was. There was a tense, coiled energy about him and Alec was the one who was covering the place, checking out of the clientele as he cut a path through the restaurant and headed to the place where she stood. Owen had, of course, been here before and he knew the layout of the hotel.

Owen was much more focused on her and her alone, and there was such an air of concentration about him as he strolled over that she could only gaze at him in wonder. Had she really been to bed with these two gorgeous men? Had she let them do that to her, tying her up and taking control of her, making her have multiple orgasms?

Yes, and it had been the best sex she'd ever had. Her body heated as the memories flitted through her mind, and she had to remind herself where she was. She had asked for a public meet on purpose.

"Thank you for joining me." She gestured at the opposite side of the banquette. She'd selected a banquette for six in order that they had plenty of space around them—a tactic she employed whenever she could—and stood by while the two men sat on that side, so that she faced them.

"Shelley's Corner is the area we consider our businessman's meeting place, by day. In the evening it has more of a pre-dinner bar atmosphere, but at lunchtime it's popular with local businesses who bring their staff and guests here to continue a meeting and get good food and good service."

It was one of her favorite places in the hotel, all dark wood and cherry red leather banquettes. It was a place where conversations could be private, and yet they were in public view. She felt safe—she felt as if she had a little bit of control in the situation. She needed that, if she was going to be direct with them.

After the waiter took their orders, however, Owen took charge.

Resting his elbows on the table he steepled his fingers under his chin and looked across at her. "You're a beautiful woman."

Monica's pulse tripped. She was unused to this kind of attention, which meant she didn't know how to react. She picked up her glass of iced mineral water. "You're trying to embarrass me."

"…especially when you come," he added.

She met his gaze, and when she did it made her pussy clench. Her hand shook and the ice in the glass chinked. She forced herself to take a sip of the water before she put it back down and responded. “Are you always this provocative?”

“Only when I want something and I can’t help myself.” There was that wicked smile of his again. He turned to Alec, who had adopted a relaxed pose. “What do you think? Or were you too busy making her come to notice the way it made her look?”

A shiver of arousal went the entire length of her spine. What was it about these two? They were so nonchalant about sex, and they seemed to be able to break down her natural reserve in seconds.

Alec nodded. “I feel deprived. I want to watch Monica’s face when she comes…although having my tongue inside her when she climaxed was pretty damn amazing too.”

When he said it, she felt him there again and her clit throbbed with longing. She crossed and uncrossed her legs, shifting in the seat as she tried to quell her body’s responses

They both watched. They knew. Heat flooded her face.

Owen rested back against the studded leather upholstery of the banquette, and once again he had the look of a Roman Emperor surveying his debauched citizens with pride.

A moment later, Alec stood up and crossed to her side of the banquette. Easing in alongside her, he nudged her closer to the wall at her other side, and rested one hand on her thigh beneath the table, stroking it back and forth.

Control was slipping away from her.

How good that felt though, she couldn’t deny it.

“I want to see your face while I make you come.”

Monica’s head snapped round and she stared at him in disbelief. “Surely, you can’t mean to—”

Before she could get the question out, Alec answered it by pushing his hand beneath her skirt and embracing the sensitive inside of her thigh, where the skin responded instantly and needled with desire under his touch.

"Oh, yes, I do." Alec's eyes shone with mischief. "I figure I have time to see it for myself before the food arrives."

Her thoughts filled with objections, but her body was screaming for more of his attention. Quickly, she scanned the room. She could see other people going about their business, laughing and chatting over their meals. In the far distance, by the entrance, people went in and out. They were all busy. Besides, his hands were under the table and right now his free hand was lifting up her skirt at the front to give him better access. The pulse between her thighs beat faster. She could scarcely think straight.

"I asked you here because I wanted to talk." She blurted that out when the original reason for requesting this meeting pressed on her conscience. It was because she had to request their discretion and talk to them about her psychometrics. Besides, this was work time to her, not private. They were blatantly ignoring that. "And we're supposed to be working."

"Everybody deserves a lunch break," Alec whispered, "and there will be plenty of time to talk, after we enjoy the first course." He leaned in and kissed her ear lobe. They had only ordered one course. He was talking about her. His hand was over the mound of her pussy and he squeezed it firmly through her underwear.

The expression on Owen's face was brooding, his attractive lips pressed firmly together in a sensuous half-smile. His eyes flickered as he watched each movement Alec made, and each reaction she gave.

She squirmed and pressed her fingers to her collarbone as she tried to keep some sense of decorum. Her hands ached to touch him back, and she fisted them, fearful of losing control in a public place. Uneasy, she glanced around the room again. Some of faces she saw were familiar—they were businessmen who came in here every week—and some of them were staff. And yet her pulse raced at the thought of doing something as outrageous as letting a man bring her to orgasm under such circumstances. They had put her in this situation and she couldn't seem to clamber her way out of it.

Torn between desire and decorum, she forced herself to look directly at them both. Alec's green eyes gleamed. Owen looked as if he was about to pounce across the table and take charge of the situation himself. They were arrogant, devious, and outrageously sexy. There was no way they were going to let her deny this. "Someone might see," she blurted. "I have a reputation to keep."

Owen shook his head. "Right now it looks as if Alec is having a really earnest conversation with you, trust me."

Trust him? Somehow that made her want to spar with him. "I don't know you well enough to trust you."

"I'd stake my reputation on this not being seen by anyone but us."

How those twinkling brown eyes of his turned her on.

When she huffed a laugh, Owen inclined his head at her. "Do you want Alec to stop?"

Alec raked one finger along the line of her pussy, pushing the damp fabric of her underwear against the sensitive, aroused skin—pushing against the very spot where she wanted to be stroked until she came.

Cursing under her breath, she shook her head. "No. I don't want him to stop."

She could hear the sense of urgency in her own voice—she could hear how husky and low her response was. Over ten years of denial had made that happen. Ten years where she'd only had wild fantasies and stolen voyeuristic moments to get off on. Brushing against the embers of other people's erotic experiences only offered her the heat, and not the total emotional and physical release she needed. That had created a tsunami of need over the years, a situation she'd kept a lid on by fastidiously avoiding contact with men and situations like this. Until now.

That tsunami was surging up, condensing into a vibrant call inside her, a call that would no longer be denied. It had taken these two men—forceful, decadent men—to push her to it, but now they had and there was no holding back.

The one small mercy was that Alec was angled so that he created a barrier between her and the rest of the restaurant. He was protecting her from view, but her level of concern was still high. Then Alec moved his fingers inside her undies and paddled them against her mound. When he bumped over the swell of her clit, she gasped aloud.

"Do it quickly," she begged. "You've got me in such a state!"

Alec gave an accusing chuckle. "Are you trying to blame me for this?" He plunged his finger deeper between her nether lips and moved it around. "You're deliciously wet, my dear. Are you saying that's our fault?"

"Hell, yes." She glared at each of them in turn. A sense of urgency combined with a heady rush. It shot through her. She began to rock backwards and forwards against the hard intrusion of his finger. Her head dropped back against the banquette, her hands clutched at her sides. She was glad of the banquette, because the way they both watched made her forget who they were and where they were, because she'd turned feral and all she was able to do was rock her hips, to meet each stroke of his thumb over her inflamed clit.

"Oh yes, the way you look…it makes me think about last night all over again." Owen grinned at her across the table. "I will never forget how hot you looked…tied up, your body bucking under me…when you climaxed."

Bloody hell. She was still vaguely aware of the voices nearby, the occasional shadows of the waiters and customers moving at the periphery of her vision. Pressure was building and her core tightened, her womb growing heavy in the moments before release.

Then Owen moved the toe of his shoe around her calf and lifted her leg. Grasping her beneath the table, he put his hand around her ankle and rested the heel of her shoe on the seat between his thighs. When he began stroking his hand up and down the back of her calf, she doubted her ability to stay quiet a moment longer, and brought her fingers to her mouth.

As her orgasm built she bit down on one knuckle, using the pain to focus her on withholding the cry of release that would otherwise be echoing around their banquette and beyond. Release barreled through her. She slumped back against the seat, her thighs shuddering.

Alec carefully rearranged her underwear, and removed his hand. To her utter mortification, he drew his hand to his lips, and licked his fingers. Across the table, Owen chuckled darkly. She had to close her eyes and press her head back against the banquette, because her whole world was spinning.

The waiter arrived with their food moments after she managed to get her skirt back into place. The waiter was familiar to her and he looked over at her longer than he normally would when he served her. Instinctively, she tidied her hair and wondered how flushed and aroused she looked. It didn't bear thinking about. The people she worked with every day would definitely notice a difference if she carried on like this. Straightening her spine she nodded and thanked him.

Thankfully, the mood returned to somewhere near normal for a business lunch as they began to eat. Monica found she was ravenous, and her club sandwich had never tasted so good. Alec had ordered a hot chicken and bacon salad, and Owen had a steak and onion baguette. As always, the food was delicious.

"I spent the morning in accounts," Alec said conversationally. He directed the statement to Monica. "Interesting team you've got up there."

Monica wondered what he was getting at, but luckily Owen stepped into the conversation.

"I missed out on that. Anything I should be aware of?"

Alec was about to speak, then paused. He obviously didn't want to say it in front of her. It felt rather awkward, and Monica knew it was because of her.

"Seems very efficient," Alec commented, eventually. "You'll have to visit before we depart."

Mention of their departure made her heart sink. Owen seemed to notice, and he reacted. Pushing his plate aside, he reached inside his jacket pocket.

"I brought a gift for you." He put a long slim velvet box on the table. It looked like the sort of thing that came from a jeweler.

"What is it?" She felt uncomfortable about accepting a gift from them.

"A token reminder of last night." He shrugged lightly and ran his finger along the top of the box. "Or a promise of things to come, perhaps?" He opened the box and turned it to face her.

Inside laid a delicate bracelet, not dissimilar to a charm bracelet. However, the catch was styled from a pair of miniature handcuffs. A promise of things to come? When she didn't move, he lifted the bracelet out and leaned across the table to put it around her wrist. She tried not to flinch.

"I thought you would be able to wear it quite discreetly, with the fastening on the inside, so it would serve as a private reminder."

"You think of everything."

"You better believe it." After he'd done up the fastening he rested his fingers on it, pressing the miniature handcuffs against the soft inside of her wrist, marking her with their impression.

Sexual energy began to surge into her even though he was only touching her wrist, but she couldn't pull her hand away, because he'd locked his gaze with hers and she saw such suggestion there that for a crazy moment she wanted to feel every ounce of his sexual power. When she gasped aloud, Owen's eyebrows drew together and he studied her with blatant curiosity.

She drew her hand away.

There was no shying away from the fact that she had to tell them.

Chapter Six

Owen was pleased by her response to the gift. As he expected, she was cautious about accepting it. Everything about her was measured, as if every step she took was carefully thought through. Yet she was tempted by the gift, and by the implication it contained.

"Was there something specific you wanted to talk about," he asked as she stared down at the miniature handcuff on her wrist. He wanted her to know that he hadn't forgotten she had something on her mind. More to the point, he was a little concerned that she was going to quiz him about their true purpose. She was a bright woman and it wouldn't take her long to notice their approach to the task was more investigational than developmental.

Monica took a deep breath then looked at them both. "I want to tell you something about me, something that I would like you to keep to yourselves."

A confession? For one moment Owen had the feeling that she was going to tell them something they didn't want to hear. Was she involved in the financial leak in some way? Had they inadvertently seduced the criminal they were looking for? "Go on."

"Do you know what psychometrics is?"

Owen frowned. "I can't say I am familiar with the term."

Alec touched his chin with his finger then pointed it at her. "Isn't it something to do with psychic ability and objects?"

Owen noticed that relief passed over her expression. She nodded. "That's it exactly. Psychometrics is a rare psychic…gift." She seemed to have trouble with the word 'gift' and paused overly long. "The person who has this ability can touch an object and experience the history of the object."

Owen frowned and sat back in the banquette. She was talking about herself. His mind began to race.

"As you've both noticed, I have a bit of an issue with personal space and with touch." She looked down at her hands, which she'd had pressed together while she launched into this confession, and now she opened her palms to them. "As you may also have noticed, I haven't touched either of you, barring our initial handshake, Owen."

Her voice faltered at the end there and she stared at him. She was afraid. Owen saw it in her eyes. She was afraid to tell them this.

"You have this ability?" He couldn't get his head around it, but he knew it was important to react evenly, to put her at ease. She was fast growing distressed now that she had told them.

"Yes, and it makes my life…challenging."

"That's incredible," Alec said. "You seriously have a psychic experience through touch?" He shook his head.

Monica reached for her glass of water and sipped at it. Her cheeks were flushed. Owen wondered how many people she had told.

Suddenly it mattered, really mattered, because she was upset about this. It was in his nature to try to put people at their ease when they were offering new information. He got more feedback that way. Above and beyond that, this was about Monica. He was deeply attracted to the woman and he had a lot of respect for the way she handled herself, especially if this psychic thing was true. "Hey, chill. You're worried about sharing personal information with us."

"Too right I am." Tension rang in her tone. "I had no choice but to tell you. That's not something I do very often. On the occasions that I've had to, I've been laughed at, or worse, branded a freak."

"That's not going to happen here," he reassured her. He wished it was the evening and they could discuss this over a good bottle of brandy. "I'm not going to lie to you. I don't quite understand what you mean. The subject is totally new to me and it's beyond my experience. But I'm always willing to listen, and I'm especially willing to listen to you."

After a moment, the tension that was evident in her posture dissipated. She took her napkin to her mouth and dabbed her lips. "Thank you."

Alec stared at her avidly. He seemed to have a better grip on what she was talking about, which bugged Owen somewhat.

"Can you demonstrate?" Alec asked.

"Kind of. I mean…I can tell you what an object tells me." She glanced across the table uneasily. "I know how ludicrous that sounds if you don't give any credence to psychic ability, but I promise you it is true."

"We're listening. Show us," Alec encouraged.

She ran her fingers along the edge of the table then moved them on to the seat between her and Alec. As she ran her fingertips over the red leather studded surface in small circles her eyelids lowered, as if she was concentrating. After a moment, she paused. Owen stretched, so he could see what she was doing. She'd splayed her palm and fingers on an area of the seating between herself and Alec. "I can tell you that we're not the first people to have touched each other intimately, in this booth."

Alec grinned. "See, and there was you putting up a struggle."

She smiled at that, which was good to see. Owen also noticed that her pupils had dilated. She was getting aroused again, and it was because of this psychic thing of hers. Her hand still ran over that spot, back and forth, around and around, as she nodded at Alec's remark. There was a light flush at the base of her neck where it met her collar bone. Her eyes widened. "Two women sat here. They'd come in here for a bit of luxury and one of them dared the other to masturbate, under the table."

Jesus, no wonder he thought she was a sensualist. Owen wasn't big on psychic matters but if what she was saying was true, she was a loaded tinderbox just waiting for a spark. And in her world, those sparks must be everywhere. No wonder she'd been cautious about touch. His thoughts raced back through the evening before and with sudden clarity he remembered how she had avoided touch and how relieved and aroused she'd been when they had elected to tie her wrists together.

"Okay, you're turning me on," Alec said, still laughing. "I only just got rid of the erection I had earlier. You're a liability, lady."

Alec's easy way worked for her, putting her at her ease. Owen had never been more glad of his partner's charm and easygoing nature. Monica looked across at him then, nervously, as if seeking his understanding.

"I can tell it's arousing you. You looked like this when we met, that made me curious."

She nodded. "I'd been in one of the suites. The handcuffs were lost property and they'd been left there. The place was buzzing with residual sexual energy. Sometimes I resist touching." She paused, and the sultry look in her eyes made his cock harden. "And sometimes I can't help myself."

Now that was something he wanted to see. "Is that suite occupied at the moment?"

Without breaking eye contact with him, she reached for the organizer she kept at her waistband and unclipped it. She scrolled through the screens then turned the device off. "No it isn't."

"I call that good luck."

She smiled. "So do I, but aren't you supposed to be coming up with ideas how to keep that suite occupied every night?"

"Touché. Right now, I'm just glad it isn't." He gestured to the waiter for the bill.

Minutes later they vacated the busy restaurant and she led them to the suite. As he walked behind her along the plush corridor Owen's fascination with her deepened. He had sensed so much beneath the surface, but he never would have guessed its source. Not in a thousand years.

When she reached the door she stopped and turned to face them. "This is the suite. Wait here, I'll check to see if there are any housekeeping staff around."

She wandered to the end of the corridor.

"Jesus, what do you make of it?" Alec asked.

Owen shook his head. "Right now it's beyond my comprehension. If I didn't know better, I'd think she was off her rocker."

"I read something about it."

Owen envied him that and the way he'd been able to follow through on her question immediately. Usually he was the one with the full deck of cards. "Thank God one of us knew what she meant."

Both of them kept their eyes on the housekeeping storage room that Monica had disappeared into while they discussed her in low voices. "If it's true, it explains a lot of the way she is, you know…that extreme sense of cautiousness about her."

"There had to be something."

Monica emerged and headed back towards them.

"I know you know this already," Owen added, "but she was worried about telling us, and it's important that we don't react badly."

Alec's eyes flickered as he acknowledged that.

Owen smiled at Monica as she approached and added in a whisper to Alec, "I might need your help with that."

"The housekeepers are on their afternoon break and this floor is pretty much done. We shouldn't be interrupted by the staff.” She looked at the door handle warily. “This is where it began.” She glanced over her shoulder as if to make sure there weren’t any guests around and they were not being watched. “I felt sexual energy sparking when I touched the door handle.”

Alec leaned over and rested his hand on the door handle. “Does that happen often?”

“No. But something happened, right here.” She swept the cardkey through the slot and Alec turned the door handle. When she stepped through the door and they followed her inside, she continued. “The couple who stayed here the night before last were intimate up against the door, before they came into the room.”

She strode across the room, delivering a list of the suite’s specifications. Owen barely glanced at it. It was her he was interested in. The Hollywood style suite merely acted as a foil for her beauty and elegance, like a suitably glamorous setting for the perfect gem. He suddenly wanted to see her in every one of the Cumbernauld chain hotels, because each one would shine with her in it.

This peculiar secret of hers went a long way in explaining why she had struck him as unique. She was an enigma. That sophisticated, slightly aloof quality she had was shot through with the sensuous nature that underpinned her character. Even the clothes she chose to wear—pristine fitted suits—were a veneer. They might be business-like on someone else, but on her they made him notice her womanly curves, her elegance, and her posture.

She stepped towards the bed, staring down at it. “He brought her the cuffs as a gift, but they knew each other well. She wasn’t shocked by them.”

Alec scrubbed at the back of his neck and looked around the room. “You could tell all of that after they had gone?”

"Yes. If I touch something, such as this," she ran her fingers along the edge of the dresser, "and they had some sexual interaction here, I get a window into the moment. They were pretty hot for each other." She turned to them, smiling as if to herself. "It's difficult for me to convey that to you."

"Not really," Owen interjected. "It's obvious you're enjoying it." When she looked pensive about his remark, he smiled.

"It's hard not to enjoy something like that, when they did."

"I can imagine." He imagined it all too well as he took in the slight flush on her cheekbones and the swell of her lower lip. Her experiences were voyeuristic. Not out of choice, but it made him wonder. Currently she was enjoying this walk through someone else's moments. Maybe she didn't always want it or enjoy it, but she was now. She'd had an attachment to those cuffs and she'd picked them up here. He recalled how she'd been when he'd pulled them out of her pocket, the day before.

One of the things that he enjoyed about sharing lovers with Alec was that he got to watch him with women. That was some turn on, especially when he could step in at any given moment and claim his share, too. Would Monica be open to that, to seeing them together as well as having them both wanting her? As each moment passed, he wanted to know. He wanted to explore all of that and watch her reactions unfold.

Alec was touching the dresser she had just touched, as if trying to engage. It made Owen think back some more. "You knew Alec and I were more than colleagues, the moment we shook hands, didn't you?"

Of course she knew. It all fit together now, like a jigsaw where he hadn't been able to find missing piece. Now it all made sense. Especially the way she'd looked when he'd given her his killer handshake. As he thought back on it, he regretted holding on to her that long, because he realized how personal that had been for her. Then again, it meant that he'd got close to her quickly, and he couldn't find it in himself to regret that.

"I knew that there was something between you, and I confess it made me outrageously curious." A warm, genuine smile lit her face.

God, she was beautiful. Owen wanted to see that smile more often. She was far too serious, but now that he knew why he could work on it.

Alec's attention was back on her, his eyes glowing vibrantly the way they did when he was really into something. He hadn't believed that she knew about them. Now he'd found out for sure.

Alec gave a husky laugh. "So you have seen images of…" He pointed over at Owen, and back at himself.

"You dropped your keys, do you remember?"

Alec nodded. "And you picked them up."

"As I mentioned, my curiosity was raging." She shifted position and leaned her shoulder up against the black lacquered post on the four-poster bed. "An object like that, something personal that is carried close to the body, something that is used again and again, often times when physical intimacy is about to occur… Well, the residual sexual energy can be mind-blowing."

"Did you find it arousing?" Owen knew it was a leading question. It was obvious, and he was getting turned on just thinking about her, thinking about him and Alec together. It hadn't put her off getting involved with them, that was for sure.

For several moments she didn't respond, but he could tell that her pulse rate had gone up. Beneath her pristine shirt and jacket her breasts rose and fell more rapidly. Her fingers twitched and she snatched at the button on her jacket to still them. “Yes. Of course I did.”

“And still you met us for dinner.” Owen couldn’t restrain his smile.

They stared into each other’s eyes, and somehow knowing how aware she’d been when she stepped into his suite the night before made it that much more delicious. He thought that revealing they were lovers was part of the arousal for him. Now, knowing that she’d addressed the realities of their bisexuality before the event—and taken such a big risk with her personal secret—made him want to make love to her again, right there and then. His thoughts darted back to the selection of items he’d picked up at an exclusive sex emporium that morning. Anticipation built inside him as he imagined bringing them into play.

“Jesus,” Alec said, and began to pace up and down, “that’s such an amazing skill, I never would have guessed.”

“No one ever does. And very few people know.” There was a deliberate, pleading look in her eyes as she glanced at them both then. “I want it to stay that way. I only told you because I had to. Things happened so fast and… well, there was no way around it.”

She was opening up. Owen wanted things to stay that way. He wanted to know all about Monica Evans. “Discretion is important to you. You can rely on us.”

Alec nodded. “Absolutely.”

Alec was quite obviously fascinated by it. Owen was too, but he was cautious. She didn’t want them to make a big deal about it or she would feel uncomfortable.

“Is it just sexual history that you can sense?” Alec quizzed.

“Mostly yes, although I have less strong images of other events if I concentrate really hard, but the sexual stuff comes through thick and fast. I have to concentrate to keep that out and block it, and that is really hard if I’m aroused.”

She shrugged. "I'm a freak." She gave a weak smile. "I've done research on it and the only reason I can find for it being strongest with sexual energy is that it's so intense, the psychic residue is stronger and that's what I tune into."

Owen couldn't resist. "Or it could be because deep down you are a very sensual and sexually-aware woman."

Quick as a flash, she was back at him, a wry smile on her face. "I thought you said I was an ice queen?"

"I knew you weren't an ice queen the moment I met you. Why do *they* think you are?"

"Oh, I don't know, maybe because I have to keep myself to myself. The people I work with have never witnessed me having a relationship and I've worked here for years."

"Why is that? Why haven't you had a relationship, I mean."

Eventually, she took a deep breath. "I opened myself to a man I cared about when I was much younger, when I was still at business college, and I was hurt by his thoughts and memories. He was with me but I was merely a replacement for someone else, the person he really wanted to be with. I'd fallen for him badly and it left me hurt and raw. I was young…" She paused. "I know now that I can't expect a normal relationship. There's always going to be some history come through. I've accepted that."

So, she'd been hurt by an ex. Owen couldn't begin to imagine thinking about any other woman when he was with her.

"For some reason," she continued, "the bondage protects me from that. It's not something I've ever tried before." An attractive flush colored her cheeks when she admitted that. "Although I was drawn to it when I experienced the residual energy of those kind of encounters."

Owen nodded. "Can't touch when you are tied up?"

"Yes, I think it might be that simple."

"If you can concentrate on other kinds of experience," Alec said, "you would be adept with investigation work. I read that the police sometimes use psychics to uncover evidence. I bet you'd be great at uncovering secrets and lies."

"Alec," Owen warned. It was pretty obvious where Alec's thoughts were leading and he didn't like it.

Alec frowned. "Sorry, mind running away with me." He stepped over to her and brushed her cheek with a kiss. "Forgive me."

Monica was sharp and she glanced at them both with caution and curiosity in her eyes. "It's a natural enough thought, but why secrets and lies? I thought you were here to help with new ideas?"

"We are." Owen raised a smile.

She cocked her head on one side, and he had a sinking feeling.

"There's something else, isn't there?" Her eyes flickered with thought. "Is it a secret, or a lie?"

Alec stared at him in way that made Owen feel uncomfortable.

"Monica has shared a private part of herself with us, surely that enables you trust her on this?"

He had a point. Owen still didn't feel right about it though. They shouldn't be burdening her with their true mission. One look at her face assured him she would figure it out if they didn't share. "I don't want to burden you with it."

Alec shot him a glance that told him he was being too guarded. He was right. But he had Monica's best interests in mind too.

"Okay, we're here because there's been some fraud. Somewhere along the line funds are going missing. Flynn Elwood denied any problems with the running of the franchise when the Board of Directors asked him about it, so we've been sent in undercover to see what we can unearth."

"Fraud?" Her expression morphed. "I'm astonished. Flynn's always telling us how well everything runs here."

"That's his story. Of course he may be denying it because he's involved."

"No, surely not?" She looked shocked.

He didn't want to destroy her faith. "Or he may be covering for a leak he can't locate either. From what we can tell he's scrambling to patch things up."

She thought about it for a few moments then nodded. "Yes, he has been working harder than ever recently, and he is stressed."

She looked at them with caution. Her loyalties were being divided, Owen could see it happening. She crossed her arms loosely and turned to one side as she thought about what had been said. Her body language reflected her mental state. This wasn't what he wanted at all.

"Were you aware that it was his wife's money that enabled their investment in the hotel?" she asked.

"Yes. Flynn Elwood doesn't just have the Board to answer to."

She tapped her chin with one finger. "Well, I don't know if I can help you find out—"

"We weren't asking you to do that," Owen interrupted. "I don't want you to feel in any way swayed by what you know about us. It just came out." He glanced at Alec, who lifted one shoulder apologetically.

Monica stared at Owen. "I know. But I'm glad you told me. It makes me feel less awkward about my own confession."

Owen smiled. "No need for you to feel awkward. I already knew you were someone very special indeed."

The atmosphere in the room altered and he noticed how she looked at him as if she wanted to believe him, but wasn't sure.

The door clicked open and a woman in a housekeeping uniform stuck her head in. "Whoops. I thought this room was vacant. Sorry, folks, I was just checking it had been done. Oh…Monica, it's you."

"Don't worry, Angie," Monica said, quickly slipping into her professional mode. "I was giving these two gentlemen a tour of the more luxurious suites. Allow me to introduce you. Mr. Stroud and Mr. Clifford are from Headquarters. Gentleman, this is Angela Burdette. Angie is one of Cumbernauld's longest serving members of staff. We've worked together since I first came here as a greenhorn from business college."

Owen watched as she encouraged the woman to step across the suite and shake hands. It was fascinating to see how little contact she made with people, whilst giving the impression of doing so. She swept her hand up to the maid's back and stepped behind her, but didn't actually touch her. While the maid shook hands with Alec and chatted with her about how long she had worked there, Owen once again made eye contact with Monica.

She smiled, tentatively. She knew he'd watched her. Owen couldn't stop watching her. A strange combination of fragility and strength was reflected in her character, and it magnetized him. She was beautiful, desirable, and unique. The rising need to possess her—to see her awash with sexual pleasure, and make her happy in every way—was getting difficult to hold back.

When Angie left, he walked over to Monica. "I don't claim to understand what you go through, but I can see it's often a trial for you."

"Yes."

"Why don't you want to touch us, the way you want to touch this place?"

"I do and I don't." A sad smile passed over her face. "I just want to be normal, I want to enjoy it the way I was able to last night, but if I get a flood of history when I want to be with someone it's…invasive."

Owen cupped her face and looked deep into her eyes. "That's fine. I only wanted to understand why." He kissed her, gently, brushing over those soft lips of hers, taking a taste and promising himself more—a hell of a lot more. "We can work around it, right, Alec?"

He observed her as she glanced at Alec, and he noticed that she looked nervous, hopeful and expectant. She wanted Alec too. That was good. That was important to him.

Alec nodded and grinned. "Too right we can."

Chapter Seven

Alec delivered his personal doubts on their situation that evening, when he and Owen were alone. They had spent the afternoon meeting the various restaurant managers. Overall it was a highly convivial session and they had ended it well fed and in good spirits, with anticipation building for their rendezvous with Monica later that evening.

While they relaxed in Owen's suite, Owen went back over the revelation of the day—Monica's psychic ability. After an hour discussing it, Alec knew that he had to bring up his concerns now, while he had the chance. As soon as he did it became blatantly obvious just how much Owen wanted Monica.

"You are spending a lot of time thinking about Monica and her psychic talent, maybe too much time?"

Wild-eyed and disgruntled, Owen Clifford was not his usual calm self. "Jesus, Alec. I thought you had more understanding."

Alec bristled. "I'm only playing devil's advocate here."

It wasn't often that Owen lost his temper, but he had surely lost it now. "I thought you had sympathy for this psychic gift of Monica's. I can't believe you're questioning it now." Owen paced the sitting area in his suite, barefoot, which was what he preferred when he was outside working hours. The fact that he was still wearing a suit and tie did have the unfortunate side effect of making him look a little bit crazy, especially when he was in a bad mood.

It was a good job that the Board of Directors couldn't see him now, Alec mused. "I'm not questioning her gift," he stated. "What I'm talking about is the whole situation. I commented on that because we've spent the last hour talking about it and although it's bloody fascinating stuff, I'm merely pointing out that we should also be talking about our work here, at least for a few moments."

Owen glared at him.

"I'm hugely attracted to Monica as well," Alec added, quickly, "don't get me wrong. I think she's perfect for us…"

As expected, that grabbed Owen's attention in a different way. His expression mellowed and the corners of his mouth lifted. "She is."

"I don't want to give up any of our time with her," Alec continued, "but I am concerned about your position here."

Owen rubbed his knuckles over his short-cropped hair, something he always did when he was worried and preoccupied. It was obvious that he didn't want any obstacles in his path to Monica. Unfortunately life wasn't that simple. He was really taken with her, they both were. Alec's mindset meant he always tried to work around obstacles, but Owen wanted to forge ahead on this, to hell with the obstacles. He'd already had to deal with her psychic ability. For a man as down-to-earth as Owen, that had been some learning curve.

Alec glanced at his watch. Monica would be with them within an hour, for the evening—hopefully for the night. He'd had to grab the opportunity to talk to Owen about what was happening, but it hadn't gone down well. He rested back in the low-slung armchair and for the first time since he'd given up smoking three years earlier, he craved a cigarette. That was bad. He only ever craved a cigarette when he felt things were getting away from him. His job as PA was to research, to think ahead, and to watch Owen's back. That's what he was trying to do now.

"The Board of Directors is watching your work closely at the moment, that's the only reason I decided to bring it up." He lifted his hands from the arms of the chair, seeking Owen's understanding.

Owen paused then gave a reluctant nod. ”Yes, you’re right there.” He undid his tie hastily, pulling it off and throwing it on a chair. Tugging at his shirt buttons he opened the collar.

Alec responded physically, his blood pumping south. The sight of his lover undressing always did that to him. Owen was a burly, direct man, and stripping off usually meant he was about to deliver an irresistible suggestion for mutual pleasure. However, this time he was distracted by more important issues and Alec quelled his instinctive response.

”Do you think I’m letting Monica distract me?” Owen asked.

Alec noticed the concern in his partner’s eyes. “It’s a borderline case, for both of us.” He gave a wry smile. “I did wonder if you were feeling a bit rebellious about the Board of Director’s attention to your work at the moment.” He delivered the comment cautiously, expecting a backlash. He got it.

Owen’s bad mood flared again. “What, you think I’m spending time with Monica because I’m avoiding an important task? Do you think I’m insane?”

Right then he looked the part. “I know you’re not, but I also know that you like to buck the trend occasionally.” He lifted his eyebrows. “That’s why you are so good at what you do.”

Owen’s expression morphed from anger to grumpiness. “Yeah, besides, I buck the trend enough by shagging my male PA while on the job, don’t you think?” Sarcasm rang in his tone.

Alec laughed. “That’s not the only reason you shag me.”

“Maybe not.” Owen shoved his hands in his pockets. He looked confused for a moment which made Alec want to hold him, but he knew that wasn’t a good idea, not right now.

Owen glanced over rather sheepishly. “So, have I missed something important?”

“I don’t think we’ve missed anything at all. I wanted to have this conversation so that we are both aware of the possibility. I’m watching out for you, Owen.”

Owen nodded. “I know. I appreciate it. She is worth it though, isn’t she?”

Alec laughed softly. That Owen wanted his approval on this indicated just how important she was. “Absolutely. I don’t think either of us could stop being involved with her, that’s not what I’m trying to say. We just need to be extra vigilant.”

Owen scrubbed his head with his knuckles again. “We’ve rattled the entire staff, just by being here. All we can do is keep looking and listening. Have you got any gut feelings about where the leak is?”

“I keep coming back to accounting because it’s the obvious one. They’ve made some alterations to the recommended system. That made me concerned. I’m going to make a copy of their database, get it onto my laptop and see if I can find anything. The financial leak could be anywhere though, cleverly concealed from the accountants. There have been a lot of refurbishments over the last year and it’s all specialist stuff.”

“Like the staff elevator?”

“Yes, and they’ve just completed a major phase of suite makeovers.” Alec shrugged. “There could be something worth looking into there, since this is a recent situation. In general the accounting systems look pretty sound.”

“We’ll have to find out who deals with the purchasing decisions on the renovation work.” Owen sat down, right on the edge of his seat with his elbows on his knees. “I had a quick look at the booking records when I came through reception this morning, and there’s a good turnover. Could be a bit better but it’s hovering at eighty-five percent occupied on average, over the current season. I'm going to go further back tomorrow."

"That's not bad at all. Like you say, we'll have to suggest ways to push it up, aim for ninety percent."

Owen studied him. "You thought about asking Monica to use her psychic ability to help us, didn't you? "

"Yes, but I didn't think that one through. I'm aware that I blundered there. I wouldn't want to put her in that position."

Owen remained thoughtful. "No. It would have to be something she offered to do."

"Let's not think about that angle. The evening is ours. There's nothing we can do until tomorrow. Let's just enjoy it."

Owen nodded but he was still distracted. Alec was, however, relieved that his partner had taken his comments on board. Neither of them wanted to give up their liaison with Monica, but neither could they afford to miss something vital, because completion of this task—quickly and successfully—was crucial to Owen's career.

Monica sat in the back seat of the big black London cab, peering through the rain-streaked windows at the passing sights. The West End of London glittered on through the rain, as ever, but it looked different tonight. That was because she was on her way back to Cumbernauld's—back to Owen and Alec. She had popped home to feed her goldfish, but Owen had only let her go if she promised to be back by eight-thirty. Nothing had really changed in this part of the world and yet everything she looked at seemed brighter and more dazzling. *It's because I am living. Really living.*

Anticipation had her body thrumming. That was a change in itself, and the fact she was truly living her life was bound to have a knock-on effect. She needed her anchors, and yet she was being set adrift from them. She took a deep, steadying breath. Had she lost all her carefully built self-defence mechanisms? It was a question that had passed though her thoughts constantly throughout the day. If things were altering she should be afraid, and she still was. A little. *I'm having fun, living for the moment, that's all it is.*

Was it an excuse? Hell, yes. But she kept telling herself she could enjoy it for as long as it lasted then pull back and return to normal. As her taxi dodged the traffic and doubts assailed her, she considered how realistic that plan was. No, her life would never be the same after they'd gone from it. A day and a half around them had assured her of that. Fundamentally, things were the same as they had been before, the hotel and her part in it. She had stepped off the path, strayed even, but her safe routine was still there and she could step right back up to it.

The one thing that really got to her was the nagging feeling that she was betraying her boss by having a private liaison with the men who had come to figure out what was going on under his roof. The truth had come out that afternoon. There was more to it. Their investigation had a trigger. That was worrying in itself. Fraud? Misappropriation of funds? And was she under investigation, too? She had been, she could see that now. In telling them her secret she had shown them she had bigger things to worry about than stealing from the company who gave her security.

Owen had assured her he wanted her to carry on as before, acting as their guide. But now she watched what went on in a different way, and—more worryingly—she wanted to help them.

As the taxi pulled in at the entrance to Cumbernauld's and the doorman stepped over to open the car door, the worries began to wisp away on the rainy night air.

All she could feel was excitement, curiosity and desire for the rendezvous ahead. *Tomorrow, I'll think about it tomorrow.*

"Good evening, Ms Evans." The doorman said, with obvious surprise.

"Evening, George. Thank you." Monica indicated the taxi driver keep the change, and slung her bag over her shoulder.

"Working late tonight?"

"Yes indeed. We have bods in from Headquarters and I'm the designated go-to person."

"Oh yes. I hear they want to have a chat with everyone, is that right?" George looked concerned. Word had got about. "It's not about job cuts is it, Ms Evans?"

"No, no I don't think so. It's about promotional ideas." It was curious that the staff thought there might be more to it. And now she'd lied, to cover for them. Each time she tried to push it away someone was sure to remind her, which was no bad thing.

Once she'd made her way through the familiar reception area with its black and white tiled floor, marble pillars and clever lighting, she felt a bit more focused. The hotel always felt different at night, the ambiance less business-like and more leisurely. It wasn't often that she got to enjoy that and as she rode up in the elevator, she observed the group of friends who shared the space, noticing how easy they were with one another. That's what she craved, and this crazy affair with two bisexual men was as near as she'd ever been. The only people she was comfortable around were her immediate family, who understood the way she was. In the short time she'd known Alec and Owen she'd had a taste of something else. Vibrant companionship and more, intimacy.

As she walked along the corridor, her fingers touched against the bracelet Owen had put on her. That took her closer to them, because they had both examined it with her in mind before it found its home on her wrist—Owen when he selected it, Alec before they gave it to her.

Owen answered the door when she knocked. His jacket and tie had gone and his shirt was open to the chest. His hair was ruffled as if he'd been working. He looked a bit stressed. But his feet were bare—that made her smile.

"Monica, oh Monica." He leaned against the frame and looked at her, keeping her waiting. "You are a sight for sore eyes."

She glanced along the corridor, wondering how professional this would look if one of the staff caught sight of her. Good thing she was supposed to be on hand for them.

"I wondered if you might stand us up," he added.

"Should I have done that?" The question was one she'd been asking herself.

"If you had, I'd have hunted you down." Lust burned in his eyes.

The emotional and physical response she experienced made her falter. Her blood rushed, her legs growing weak under her. Once he'd delivered that comment, however, he reached out and put his arm around her back, ushering her in. With his free hand, he took her handbag and deposited it on a table that stood inside the door.

"Close your eyes," he instructed.

Surprised, she paused.

"Close them…"he repeated, and it was a total command.

When she did, he stood at her back with his hands covering her eyes. It was strange, but compelling. She was in his hands, literally.

"Step forward, I'm right with you."

Monica moved and as she did so she was soon breathless with sensation, because the unusual experience of having her vision obscured made her desire to touch things flare wildly. How strange, she considered. Owen did things that were natural to him but keyed in to her needs, needs that even she was unaware of. He'd contained her hands when she needed that, and now he made her want to touch things, which—ultimately—she might have to. *Not ready yet*.

The temptation was there though, however briefly. Of course the fact that Owen was so close against her back had its own appeal.

"Ready for your surprise?" The way he whispered that against her ear made her shiver with anticipation.

"Only just." She rested her hand briefly against his where it covered her eyes. She liked his hands there, taking away one of her senses. If only he could take away the sixth sense that blighted her life.

"So sensual," he whispered, and kissed the side of her face before he removed his hands.

Several black and purple bags were set out on the same table that'd had an aphrodisiac menu arranged on it the night before. The bags bore the name "Mistress" and had a silhouette illustration of a woman trailing a whip in one hand and a chain in the other. That gave a pretty big hint at what was inside the bags. "It looks as if you've had quite a shopping trip."

From the corner of her eye she saw that Alec was in the adjoining room, on the phone.

"Just a couple of things I thought you might like." Owen made the comment then stepped behind the table and looked at her over the shopping bags, as if urging her to consider the goodies.

As she stared over she thought about the diamante handcuffs from the Hollywood suite. The night before she'd been bound in her own stockings and she recalled how good it felt, being unable to touch, and yet being thoroughly exposed and vulnerable in her sexuality. Submitting to them that way had brought her pleasure beyond anything she'd ever felt before. She remembered, too, Owen's fingers on her wrist at lunchtime, when he latched that bracelet together and called it a promise of things to come.

What was in the bag?

Owen rested his hands on the table and gazed at her before he reached in and lifted something out. The item was wrapped in tissue paper. He unwrapped it carefully and pulled it free, showing it to her.

Monica found herself inexorably drawn towards the table so she could get a better look at whatever that was in his hand.

There were cuffs, two soft black leather cuffs. Between them was not a chain though, but a straight piece of metal. When he saw her looking at it, he manipulated the object and the metal lengthened.

“Interested?”

“I am. What is that?”

“It’s a restraint device.” Owen lifted the item over his head, one hand on either cuff, indicating how the wrists could be spread apart by the cuffs.

Monica’s lips parted and she gave the softest of laughs as she realized how absolutely perfect the decadent bondage item was for her. When he saw her pleasure, he put it down on the table, rolling it towards her.

“Nice,” Alec commented when he joined them from the room beyond and saw the gift.

Monica picked it up and moved her fingers along the cool metal and the soft black leather wrist straps. It took a moment for her to realize Owen had lifted a second such item from the other bag.

“These can also be used on ankles, to spread the legs.”

Monica’s skin raced, every nerve ending sparking with electricity as she pictured herself restrained at wrist and ankle with these things. If she was naked, she would be exposed in every way, vulnerable, accessible, and at their complete command. She could scarcely stand up straight thinking about it, and had to rest the tips of her fingers on the table so as not to stagger. It made her a teeny bit afraid. Mostly she wanted to assume whatever position they chose to put her in. Her body was clamoring for more of what she had gained before, to be used and released through submission to them.

A moment later the sound of a champagne cork popping jolted her from her trance. Alec was busy pouring them a drink. When he held out a glass to her, she stepped over to collect it and swigged back some of the frothy wine to ease her nerves.

Owen accepted his drink and lounged in the captain's seat. He never took his eyes off her. She took another sip of the champagne, and ran her fingers over the cuffs. As she did, sexual energy funneled into her. "Oh."

She was about to withdraw her hand when she felt the source. Owen. She glanced across at him. He lifted his head, watching her.

"You handled them in the shop, and you thought about this moment while you did that."

"True." The fascination in his expression made her want to say more.

She pressed the soft leather between her fingertips. "The image I am seeing is a decadent looking shop. It has red velvet curtains and cedar wood cabinets. On top of the cabinet there are velvet cushions with black tassels at each corner. These are used to display the erotic bondage items that are kept in the cupboards below."

Owen nodded. His expression had grown serious. He wanted to know more.

"You handled this and you imagined me in the restraint." She had to pause, because of the rush she got. He'd pictured her on her hands and knees, naked. He stood behind her, with his erect cock in his hand. She drew her fingers away and looked at him.

"And?" He seemed to be waiting expectantly, and she put the glass down on the table.

Looking at him, she responded. "You got a hard-on, and you were eager to get back to the hotel."

"Yes, and I've been anticipating it ever since." He beckoned her closer. "All the way through lunch, and afterwards."

She stepped nearer and, as she did, she studied the enigma that he was. Confidence oozed from every pore—confidence to the point of arrogance. He looked at her as if she was his possession. It shouldn't have, but those very facts made her want to fall to her knees and beg for his attention. Either that or run. Which would it be? She didn't have long to consider the question because once again he took charge.

"Are you ready to begin?"

She stood in front of him, waiting for his command. She nodded.

"Strip," he instructed.

With shaking hands she removed her clothing, carefully laying each item over the back of a nearby chair. This was different to last night. Alec had gone to take shower, leaving them alone. When she got down to her underwear, she paused.

His hands embraced the arms of the captain's chair he sat in, as if he was pacing himself. Then he lifted one finger and pointed at the bra. It was instruction enough. The way he sat, so expectant, so ready to pounce, told her everything she needed to know. She reached around and unhooked her bra, slowly taking it off.

"Touch your breasts for me, show them to me."

His eyes flickered as she followed his instruction and cupped her breasts in her palms. She manipulated them, and as she did memories of the night before flashed through her mind. A breathless moan escaped her mouth, and she squeezed both nipples between thumb and forefinger, eager for the dart of pleasurable pain that action sent from her breasts to between her thighs, where the pulse in her clit thudded wildly.

When she made that sound he stood up, and reached for one of the restraints, readying it. “Enough.”

Her hands fell to her sides, which left her breasts aching for more.

While he contemplated her, the metal bar glinted in his hands. He bristled with barely contained power. “I want you naked. Everything else comes off, now.”

Monica’s hands shook as she reached for the zipper on her skirt. She wanted to do it, but the idea that she followed a man’s instructions regarding getting undressed—a work colleague, no less—went against everything she thought she would ever do. At that moment she was under his command though, and doubted that she could force herself to argue. Kicking off her heels, she shuffled her skirt off then ran her thumb under the band on her lace undies, pausing.

Owen lifted one eyebrow.

When she shoved her underwear down the length of her legs and stepped out of the abandoned lace, his mouth moved in an appreciative smile. From top to toe, he examined her. With a shaky intake of breath, she kicked off her heels then lifted one foot and placed it on a chair, so that she could roll her stocking down her leg.

Before she’d even got one stocking off, he’d sauntered over and rested up against the table next to her, eyeing her while she took off the stockings. When she changed to the other leg he reached in and stroked his fingers along the seam of her bare pussy. The brief, provocative touch sent her nerve endings crazy. It was hard to keep undressing, but she had to. Once entirely naked, she dropped the second stocking and presented herself to him.

He held the slim metal bar out in front of her, his fist wrapped around it. Monica melted. Everything about him suggested strength and control. It was what she had to be like every day of her life to keep her psychic self in order, but handing that over to him was an experience way beyond anything she might have imagined. It was hard, but it was also the biggest temptation she'd ever known.

"There are so many reasons why I shouldn't do this," she whispered as she put her left wrist into the leather cuff.

Owen did up the metal buckles that held the soft leather in place. "It's also what you want, what you crave. You showed me that." Nodding at her right wrist, he closed the leather over it. "Whether you intended to or not is debatable." He smiled as he buckled her in.

When it was in place, he wrapped his fist around the middle between her hands, and lifted it, stretching her arms over her head. The movement was so sudden and so unexpected that she gasped aloud. Her shoulders rolled and locked, her breasts lifting with the movement. Tension beaded down her spine.

He stared deep into her eyes. "This morning, when I thought you couldn't stand to be touched…that really messed with my head."

There was a pained note to his voice that made her ache.

His gaze drifted down to her breasts and back up to meet hers and locked. "Because what I really wanted to do was explore every inch of you."

Instinctively, her fingers curled into palms when he mentioned 'touch' but her hands were totally excluded from the scenario by the leather cuffs on the metal rod. He noticed what she did though, glancing at her hands, before he stroked her jaw softly with his free hand. "I'll keep you safe."

With that he lowered the bar and used it to lead her towards the bedroom door. The tug on her wrists was delicious, and the fact that he was leading her made her body grow ever more ready for him. He stood her by the bedroom door, turned her around and eased her back against it. Lifting the bar, he latched it over the coat hook that was there. She was pinned there.

"I'm going to indulge my need to explore you now." He stroked her jaw again then wrapped his hand round her throat. He looked into her eyes as he did so. It was as if he demanded her trust. Monica nodded, lowering her eyelids. His hand splayed at her collarbone then he led one finger between her breasts, following her breastbone down. As he did so he moved in and kissed her. The thrust of his tongue into her open mouth made her reach for him and her back arched against the door. Owen drew back, making her reach again before he thrust his tongue deeper, claiming her and owning her.

Each time she felt the thrust of his tongue in her mouth her centre ached for him to thrust there too. The heat between her thighs had built, and she could feel the sticky tracts of her own juices marking her inner thighs. Her heart soared, the rush of raw emotion she felt for the way he handled her entwined with the real physical desire she felt. All of that was bound up in the certainty that he would take her and make her his.

His hands closed around her breasts, his thumbs grazing the hard nubs of her nipples. That launched such an intense barrage of stimulation that she moaned into his mouth and swayed. Breaking with the kiss, Owen looked down at her, studying her while he squeezed the mobile flesh of her breasts in his hands. The intense scrutiny made her shiver and shift within her restraint.

Then his hands were on her thighs, to either side of her pussy, and as he dropped to a squat in front of her he ran his thumbs down her seam to open her up. Inside a heartbeat, his mouth had covered her clit. The metal restraint creaked when her body jerked against the door. He stroked his tongue up and down over her clit. She was so sensitive that she felt sure she would have pushed him away with her hands on his shoulders, had she been free. It was almost too much, and when his tongue rode back up, there was nothing she could do but submit. “Owen, Owen, please.”

Back and forth his tongue went, and his hand stroked around her thighs and down her legs to clasp her calves, it was as if he couldn’t hold enough of her. Her clit thrummed, and a wave of release hit her. She’d barely inhaled, and his fingers were exploring her folds. When she glanced down she found him looking up her with dark eyes, possessive eyes.

He rose to his feet and held her waist in both hands as he looked at her. “So much beauty, so hidden away. It’s a crime, Monica.”

The intense pleasure she found in the simple compliment made her glance away and she had to bite her lower lip in order not to deny what he’d said. She wasn’t used to it, and her reaction was to deny it, to walk away.

“Good girl,” he added, as if he knew how hard she found this. There was a wicked flash of humor in his eyes. He was right up against her, and when he drew away she leaned into him and kissed his collarbone where his shirt was open, tasting the salt on his skin, kissing his throat gratefully. Her body trembled as she considered what he might do with her. With her wrists bound and split, it was like a step into the unknown, but it was because her wrists were bound that she felt able to rest her cheek against his shoulder and show him how much she wanted him. “You make me crave what I shouldn’t have,” she whispered.

“It’s not wrong to want these things, Monica. I obviously need to educate you.” He lifted her chin.

It was true, he did need to educate her. What if she liked it too much, though? In a matter of days, they’d be gone.

"Nice arrangement." It was Alec, and he walked over to them, wearing nothing but a towel around his waist. The testosterone in the atmosphere had doubled, and it made Monica feel outrageously horny. Owen had stimulated her, and now her body begged for more. Alec's chest and abs gleamed, his skin still damp from the shower. His blond hair, usually spiked, was smoothed back over his head, giving him a devilish look.

"Although I think you are a little underdressed," Alec added. He folded his arms across his chest as he contemplated her.

Owen did the same. "Perhaps you are right. I've got just the thing."

He strode off and returned a moment later with the second restraint. Alec unhooked her and led her to the centre of the room, where a deep wine colored rug bearing the Cumbernauld logo stood at the end of the bed. Alec stood her in the middle of the rug.

"On your hands and knees," Owen instructed.

She dropped and Alec moved with her, easing the rod that held her wrists apart onto the rug. He looked so deliciously decadent with that towel around his waist and his damp limbs gleaming.

"Knees apart," Owen said, from behind her.

She glanced back over her shoulder. With an almost lazy movement, he opened his shirt buttons with one hand, the metal restraint held aloft in the other. Doubt riddled her. If she spread her legs as well, she would be totally at their mercy. Then he knelt on one knee beside her, and stroked his hand between her thighs.

When her head dropped and her eyes closed, he moved his hand from one side to the other, walking her knees apart. Shuffling, she followed his guide. A moment later she felt the cool leather against her ankles.

"An irresistible temptation," Alec commented and pushed his fingers through her hair before he rose to his feet.

It was only as they walked around her, both of them staring at her, that she realized how lewdly displayed she was—naked, on her hands and knees, with her legs and arms splayed apart by the restraints. Unable to shift position, her breasts hung down and her entire rear end was on display. She tried to be aware of where they were, but the way they looked at her was so overwhelming that she hung her head, grateful when her hair trailed down on either side of the face.

"If you feel uncomfortable, in anyway, just say so," Owen instructed.

Monica managed to nod her head.

Then they both walked away, and left her that way.

Chapter Eight

Somehow, being left there, naked and on her hands and knees—so vulnerable and exposed—made Monica's heart race even quicker, so fast that her breathing quickly became erratic. She seemed to see herself from all angles, from above and behind as they wandered nonchalantly away from her.

Swallowing down her nerves, she peeped up at them through her hair.

Alec returned to the champagne bottle and refilled the glasses. When she glanced over, she could see that Alec had dropped his towel. There was something so deliciously decadent about watching him reveal the solid muscular physique of his buttocks that she whimpered aloud. His gorgeous arse was as fit as the rest of him, and should have come with a wet-knickers warning. As he turned to one side she could see that his cock was already long and hard. When he clutched his balls in his hand briefly, she had to tell herself not to drool. He reached for the glass of champagne.

Owen had kicked off his shoes and she saw his shirt drop to the floor. Then he walked back towards her, squatted down in front of her, and lifted her chin with one finger. With a swift move he brought a glass to her lips. She looked into his eyes as she sipped gratefully at the drink he offered her.

When he returned to the table, he shed his trousers and shorts.

Monica's breath caught in her throat, because when he did that Alec acted on it.

"Looking good, my man," he commented, then dropped to his knees in front of Owen. He placed his hands flat to Owen's thighs, anchoring himself there as he licked

Owen's cock from base to crown before swirling his tongue around the swollen head.

It was then that she realized they had positioned her where she would see this happening. The knowledge startled her, but then she knew it had to be done. She had known they were lovers, but witnessing the evidence was the most arousing thing Monica had ever seen. Owen stood tall and straight, his feet widely placed, the muscles in his thighs and belly taut as Alec fellated him. She watched eagerly as Alec tugged on Owen's balls and Owen grunted, his hand resting briefly over Alec's head, a gesture suggesting encouragement. Alec knew exactly what do, and he worked that cock in and out of his mouth, building speed, maintaining the rhythm and gently squeezing and tugging Owen's balls as he did so.

Owen's head dropped back, his eyes closing, the muscles in his neck standing out like rope. His hips jerked, and she saw that Alec had wrapped his hands round the erect shaft of his lover's cock and concentrated his action on the head. Moments later, Owen came. She saw Alec swallow, then pull free. Grabbing his shirt from the floor, he wiped Owen off.

"Got some more for the lady?" Alec said with a distinctly teasing expression as he wiped his lover's thighs. Even while he spoke, he was stimulating Owen at the base of his cock. Owen looked over at her with dark, lust-filled eyes. He smiled her way and she felt it then, the symbiosis, the mutual willingness to share and enjoy.

"Oh I've got plenty for Monica. In fact, you've just made sure I'll last even longer for our beautiful guest."

Even longer. The idea of him plowing into her made her shiver. Her body was so desperate for it and so keyed up, she could scarcely imagine being able to stand it. Meanwhile she was riveted to the image of the two men together. Alec's cock was long and hard and arced out from his hips like a beautiful piece of sculpture. Yet he was intent on arousing Owen, as if his own pleasure was secondary to that of the man he was servicing. In the pit of her belly there was an ache of longing that swelled as she looked at Owen's cock growing hard again. His erection had barely subsided, but in answer to Alec's comment about her, it was right back.

Owen took it in his hand and stroked it up and down in a lazy movement as he approached her. Alec had risen to his feet and was now standing in front of her, observing. Owen stood behind her, and she became increasingly aware of how exposed her rear end was, every part of her on display to him. Her body reacted, her sex tightening. When it did, moisture ran down between her folds, maddening her. She swayed, her breasts dangling lewdly. "Please," she begged, desperate for relief.

"Please what, Monica?" Owen asked from behind her. "I need to know how much you want it."

Monica cursed under her breath. Acting on instinct, she rose up onto her knees, tossing her hair back as she did so. Gazing up at Alec where he stood with his hand riding up and down on his shaft, she locked eyes with him. His hand stilled. She moved forward, the burn of the carpet on her knees making her nerves ragged. First she rested her cheek against the hot surface of his shaft, moving her face against him adoringly. Then she licked him, eagerly tasting the salty, fecund taste of his cock. When she ran her tongue up and down the arced shaft from where his fist was anchored around the base, to the head, he growled in his throat.

"Give it to me," she whispered. She opened her mouth, and he directed his cock to it. Taking the swollen head into her mouth, she closed her eyes and sucked, tasting him, her tongue lapping around the head before she shifted and took as much length into her mouth as she could.

The action made her even hornier, and hearing his response made sweat break out on her back. She saw that his balls had tightened and lifted, and felt his cock grow harder still as she worked it in her mouth. When she glanced up at him the tight muscles of his abs were standing out, his belly a hard rock of tension. His eyes glittered, his eyebrows drawn down as he concentrated on her.

"Okay, I'm convinced." It was Owen and he was at their side.

Ducking down, he picked her up with his arms locked around the waist. Manhandling her easily he carried her to the bed. It was so unexpected that she cried aloud, then laughed, drunk on the moment. When he got her to the bed he positioned her so that she was on her hands and knees again. He put her facing into the room, hands right at the end of the bed. The footboard gave her something to butt up against, and leverage.

A moment later he knelt on the bed behind her stroking his fingers down the exposed lips of her pussy. Her eyes closed.

"What is it that you need?"

"You, inside me."

"Here?" He pushed two fingers inside her, scissoring them to stretch her open.

"Oh, oh…" Her head lifted. When she opened her eyes she saw that Alec had followed. While he looked at her, his fist rode up and down the slick shaft of his cock, riding easily where her mouth had lubricated it. At her back, she heard Owen rip open a condom packet. All of it impacted on her senses, making her wild and restless in her restraints, her body undulating, her nipples hard and jutting.

Alec tipped her chin up with one finger. "That's a lovely mouth you have there, very skilful too."

It was subtly delivered but the invitation was there—two men filling her, at once. It was so enticing that an urgent pang of need rang through her. Shame flooded her sex when she realized that she wanted them both, that she was hungry for this outrageous debauchery. How delicious that feeling of shame was. She welcomed it because it made her feel so damn good.

Alec's cock was so close to her lips and it oozed a drop of semen that tempted her to taste and enjoy. She ran her tongue along her lips to let him know she wanted more.

"Sure you can take it?"

Monica wanted it, but she wondered if she could take it all at once. "I want to try."

He directed his cock to her lips with his free hand. As soon as she took him into her mouth again she felt Owen entering her, his thumbs splaying her folds open as he thrust inside her sex. It was too much at first and her body was overwhelmed by the sensation of being filled, completely. Then she found her rhythm, swallowing a good length of Alec's cock and an intake of breath on each of Owen's thrusts. She wanted it all, she wanted to be filled and used and sated in every way.

"That's it," Alec whispered, panting.

Owen was right against her back and he rubbed his hand over her breasts, his fingers demanding against her peaked nipples. All of it made her feverish, weak and agitated all at the same time. She was so thoroughly debauched. But it was what her body had craved ever since she knew they were lovers and that they shared women—to be penetrated by them both. On the unforgiving loop of Owen's thrusts her body went taut then limp, capable only of absorbing each wave of sensation.

Relentlessly, Owen worked himself in and out of her, living up to his promise to last. Long before he came, Alec whispered a warning and pulled back. She whimpered, but the sight of his distended cock ready to blow held her attention. The fact that it so accurately mirrored the one that filled her sex was pure joy. She could watch and experience all at once.

"Look at me," Alec requested.

When she did so, he jerked his fist along the slick length of his cock and spurted over her neck and breasts. The act was so deliciously obscene and yet so right and true that she cried out and began to come very quickly, her body lifting up, her sex clenching and spasming.

All the while Owen worked into her, repeatedly, his hands manipulating her buttocks, squeezing them together then pulling them apart as he thrust deep against her centre.

"Coming soon, lover," he whispered at her back.

She nodded, acknowledging his warning. Bracing herself, her back arched. The tender, sensitized walls of her sex were still in spasm around the rock hard line of his cock and when he finally let rip, she felt the extreme pressure of his crown wedged against her cervix. The sensation let loose another wave of release, another climax barreling through her.

It was nearly two in the morning, they were sprawled together in Owen's bed, and Monica was apparently refusing to close her eyes. Alec smiled to himself. She was like a kid at Christmas. It was as if she thought it wouldn't happen if she went to sleep. He never needed much sleep, so he was enjoying watching her fight it.

"Not tired?" he queried.

"Yes." She laughed softly.

When he looked at her in the lamplight it occurred to him that he'd never seen anyone look less like an ice queen. She was stretched out on the bed on one side, supine against the pillows. Owen was behind her, and he trailed his fingers along her body slowly, searching out her sensitive places as she half dozed on the bed between them.

"How long do you think you'll be working here?" she said, and the question was tentatively asked.

Owen replied quickly, and made brief eye contact with Alec as he did so. "At least another few days."

"I should really go home," she responded. "I need clothes for tomorrow."

"You should have brought some when you went home for your fish."

"I wasn't sure…but I should bring more into the office if I'm going to be doing this while you are here." A naughty smile passed over her face.

"Bring them here." Owen said, lazily. He clamped his hand on her, possessively. That intrigued Alec. He had never seen Owen so fascinated with a woman, but then again, he could understand it. She was fascinating. The caution and reticence that was in her because of her psychic ability was tempered by a deep sensual character. She was keen and eager for physical experience now that she had established the boundaries. Like an unexplored territory, she was nothing like any other woman he'd known.

It would take a long time to discover everything about her, and piecing it all together was something he would very much like to do. He had no doubt that Owen felt the same. He was currently nuzzling her neck while he spooned her from behind, his hand locked over her hipbone and holding her against him.

"No!" Monica declared. "I'm having to dodge the housekeeping staff as it is." Again she laughed softly. She looked happy and Alec liked it. There had been an obvious sense of loneliness about her when they first met, and it was gradually fading.

"I keep a change of clothes in the office, which was just as well, yesterday." She flashed them an accusing stare. "I'll order a taxi, soon."

Alec reached over and massaged her wrists gently where the leather cuffs on the restraint had been. She didn't stop him. Instead she looked at him from under lazy eyelids, and smiled. He took that as a sign that he was handling her correctly. He avoided touching her palms and fingers. Glancing down at them he grew curious. "What if you wear gloves?"

"It doesn't really help."

"You've tried?"

"Yes. I've tried everything." She lifted one shoulder in a half shrug. "I can't get rid of it. "

"You just have to work around it," he offered, moving his fingers gently on her forearms.

"Yes." A pensive look had taken up residence on her face. "Only I've never met anyone who wanted to help me with it, outside of my sisters. I mean I've never had a lover who wanted to try to help me with it, the way you two have."

Alec didn't want to comment on that. "You have sisters?"

"Two, both younger."

"Are they like you, are they gifted in this way?"

"We are all psychics, but in different ways. Holly gets strong feelings about people and events. Faye can communicate with ghosts."

"Seriously?"

Owen lifted his head. "You girls must be fun at parties."

"You'd think so, wouldn't you?" She gave a wry smile. "We learnt our lesson on that score as kids, years back. It's nothing but trouble, believe me. We keep it to ourselves, mostly. Too many bad experiences. People either don't believe it or laugh or treat you as a freak…or worse."

Worse? What was worse? Alec wondered.

She fell quiet.

Owen had moved his hand to cup her breast. Alec watched the nipple tighten and peak before his eyes. She was so responsive. Just watching that made him hard. As her eyelids lifted, he saw that her pupils had dilated. She wriggled her hips.

Owen lifted his head. “Are you sure we can’t convince you to stay?”

“Hmm, maybe. I’ll have to get up early and shoot home before work.”

“I’ll set an alarm.” He walked his fingers down to the mound of her pussy and tapped them there. “Or you could pop home at lunchtime.”

“It’s a deal.” She stretched, her legs straightening, the toes pointing.

“In that case, can I interest you in some more hot sex?” Owen asked. After he delivered the question, he made eye contact. Alec grinned. He was already hard. He didn’t need any more encouragement. What did Owen have in mind?

Monica gave a pleasurable sigh.

“That sounded like a yes to me. Alec, did that that sound like a yes to you?”

Alec nodded. “Definitely a yes.”

Alec moved his fingers, squeezing then between her thighs. She wriggled, the muscles in her thighs tightening, crushing his fingers. “That’s a powerful grip you’ve got there, madam.”

“That’s because you are both turning me on.”

Owen grinned. “Anything special we can interest you in?”

Monica stretched again, and her cheeks were adorably flushed. She looked at Alec from under her lashes then glanced over her shoulder at Owen. “You know what I’d really like…”

Alec’s attention sharpened.

Owen nudged her. “Go on, we’re dying to know.”

“I’d like to see more of what I saw earlier. I’d like to watch you two together.”

Alec caught Owen’s glance.

Owen simmered with the dark sexuality and his eyes flickered, interest flaring in them. This was a first. They’d never shared a woman who actually asked to see them together before. Sometimes it just happened, as it had earlier that evening when he’d sucked Owen off.

Monica had liked it, and she wanted to see more.

Chapter Nine

I'd like to watch you two together. What had got into her?

It was as if their sexual confidence had invaded her. Either that, or the way they nurtured and encouraged her allowed her to be more open about deep, hidden desires, sexual fantasies that had risen to the surface when she had met them. Whatever the reason, the desire to see their bodies entwined that way was overwhelming. Monica had blurted it out, but now that she saw how keen they were, she realized that she'd stimulated something they both wanted. Had they been waiting for her to indicate that she was interested in that, and that she wouldn't turn away?

They rolled together on the bed, all wandering hands and lunging hips as they made full contact. Their lean strong muscles flickered in the lamplight. Owen's cock was rock hard. Alec moaned loudly when it was pressed against his hip. Monica's sex clenched. She was mesmerized. In the hazy midnight hours, high on pleasure and erotic adventure, the moment seemed surreal yet oddly vivid. She didn't want to miss a moment—she didn't even want to blink or breathe—so that she could thoroughly absorb every little detail.

"On your front," Owen ordered, taking charge. He stood up, reached into the bedside drawer and threw a tube of lube and a condom packet onto the bed. The way he stood there—commanding yet nonchalant, blatantly at ease in his naked form while he prepared to fuck his male lover—made Monica wriggle back against the stacked pillows to get a better view, anticipation making her blood race.

Alec obediently rested face down on the bed, watching Monica watching him, a half-smile captured in his expression.

"Alec loves an audience," Owen commented as he climbed over him and shoved Alec's legs apart with one knee, his body agile and rapid.

"I noticed that earlier," she responded, and winked at Alec.

Alec growled at her but there was approval in his eyes. He wanted her to be like this with them. That sent a rush of crazy emotions through her. She was high on this, high on the idea of being with these two, and being wanted by them.

"Oh yes, you're tuning in to all his pervy little fantasies." Owen reached for the condom.

"Really?" She watched as he rolled the rubber onto his cock, fascinated.

Owen nodded and his hands roved over Alec's back, eagerly, before he grabbed the lube he'd dropped on the bed. He spread the slick fluid on his sheathed erection, smoothing it over the engorged head of his cock, then moved his hands down and between Alec's buttocks.

Alec's body moved against those lubed fingers. His expression became intense, his features contorted, his head lifting and his body writhing. When he gave a long guttural moan she knew that he'd been penetrated. The response she felt was raw, her own sense of need building rapidly.

"Ready for me, huh?" Owen gave a low laugh, and arranged his body over his lover's. He kissed the back of Alec's neck while he began his entry, a tender gesture that offset the more direct contact below.

Alec looked as if he was holding his breath while awaiting the penetration.

Owen groaned as he worked his way in and the muscles of his shoulders stood out in stark relief. From her place against the pillows she watched, and she burned up with the sight of it. She could see from the tension in his body that each move he made fuelled his need. It made her so horny that she found she was touching herself, without even thinking. Her fingers moved over the sensitive flesh of her sex, alternately stroking her clit and thrusting a finger inside as she watched.

"Open your legs," Alec instructed, when he saw what she was doing. "Let us see you."

She whimpered, suddenly self-conscious. The view was so intoxicating that she'd scarcely been aware of her own actions—actions stimulated by that view.

"Fair's fair," Alec teased, "if you want to watch us, we want to watch you."

The idea of them doing that together while watching her sent her into overdrive. She rubbed herself faster, and when Owen pulled out and she saw the length of his latex covered cock easing back between Alec's taut buttocks, she couldn't resist. She opened her legs wide and put her feet flat to the bed, knees drawn up. Easing back against the pillows she arranged herself so that she was propped up in the corner of the bed—in the perfect position to view them, while being viewed by them.

"Oh yes, that's good," Alec said, and remained faced in her direction. His eyes had narrowed to dark slits and a deep, pleasured groan escaped him each time Owen eased his cock back in. Then Alec shoved his hand under himself to hold his own cock. Panting rapidly, he began to undulate against the bed in time to Owen's thrusts. When his upper body lifted, she saw his long, hard cock was in his fist and he was riding it against the bed. The muscles in his neck were taut with effort.

At his back, the concentration on Owen's face was intense. The way he measured strides, taking care with his lover, his hand riding up and down Alec's flank as he invaded his rear end—it was the hottest thing that she had ever seen.

"Oh god, yes, right there." Alec threw the comment over his shoulder in a low voice between gritted teeth.

Owen flung his head back and sweat gleamed on his forehead.

They moved in deep thrusts at each other's bodies, their expressions reflecting every action and reaction. Sweat gleamed on their skin as their breaths began to come in short grunts. And they were both keeping an eye on her because she was rubbing her clit hard now, her legs spread, her body totally keyed. On the edge of her orgasm, her breath trapped in her throat, she moaned and bit her lip and came, her body shuddering with release.

Owen's hips jerked frantically, and his eyes closed.

A stream of curses spilled from Alec's mouth. His hips pumped slower and slower until he stilled.

Three hours later, Owen stared down at the piece of paper in his hands in disbelief. The note had obviously been shoved under the door of the suite during the night, and he spotted it when he got up that morning. While Alec rang for breakfast from room service and Monica was in the shower, he took a look at it.

"This has got to be some kind of joke," he whispered under his breath.

Back off. Tell the compeny who hired you that everything is running well at Cumbernauld's. Otherwise you will regreat poking your noses in here.

He heard movement behind him and glanced over his shoulder. Luckily it was only Alec. He didn't want Monica to see this.

"What's up?" Alec peered over, astute as ever to Owen's moods.

Owen held out the note. "This. It has to be a joke."

Alec took it and stared down the paper with an amazed expression on his face. "Unbelievable, someone has been watching too many episodes of Colombo."

"It has to be a joke, really, doesn't it?" Owen didn't like it.

"A joke, or else the source has a talent for stealing money but is crap at delivering a good threat. That is some creative spelling there too." Alec turned the piece of paper over and examined the back of it. "Regular printer paper. Could be from anywhere in the hotel."

Owen stared at the piece of paper and he forced a laugh. Even so, it unnerved him. There was something distinctly odd about it.

"It concerns me though," Alec added. "Do you think the person has figured out that we are actually investigating?"

"Could be."

"How did they find out?" Their eyes locked. The only one who knew was Monica.

"Lucky guess," Owen responded, tersely.

Alec nodded then his eyebrows lifted. "Hey, we might actually be running them out of the long grass."

That was true. "It would have to be someone pretty ditzy to think this would actually concern us."

Concerned he was, though.

The sound of Monica humming to herself in the bedroom alerted him to her presence. He folded the piece of paper up and strode over to the armchair where his jacket had been left the night before. He pushed it into the inside pocket quickly, before she could notice what they were doing. Glancing back over his shoulder at Alec, he put one finger to his lips.

Alec nodded.

When she joined them, a few moments later, she was wearing one of the bathroom robes. "I've been thinking," she said. "If I can help you, you know…" She put her palms together then apart, indicating that she meant via touch, via her psychic ability, "…I'd like to do that."

"Are you sure?" Alec got in there before Owen could, as if aware that he was still worried about the note.

"Yes, I am sure."

Her smile was the true gift because it was so different from the way she had been the morning before. Owen felt an immense sense of gratitude.

"I'll have to liaise with my staff first. What are your plans for later this morning?"

"I'd like to get back into the accounts office," Alec said. "If that's okay with you Owen?"

Without hesitation, Owen nodded. Alec had not been satisfied with the way things were being run there. It made sense to pursue it.

"I'll see if I can work my charm on Miss Moody." He grinned.

"Miss Moody? Do you mean Jane Mooney?" Monica asked.

"You don't think it fits?"

She thought about it and after a moment she chuckled. "Well, now that you mention it…"

"It's not something I would normally do, but I'm trying to fit in here at Cumbernauld's of London," he said, with obvious sarcasm, "where inappropriate nicknames seem to be *de rigueur*."

Monica laughed and pointed her finger at him accusingly. "You're bad."

Alec shrugged. "I thought you knew that already."

Owen observed the exchange, and he liked the way they were around each other.

Alec glanced back at him. "What about you?"

"I need to meet with our 'fearless leader', Flynn Elwood, this morning," Owen replied with a sardonic smile—another inappropriate nickname for the roll call. The note he'd received was still bugging the hell out of him, and he was going to see if he could find out who'd sent it. "Monica, can you stick with Alec today?"

"Yes, of course."

Alec closed in on Monica. "I plan to make a copy of the accounting system they are using. If you are willing to come along with me…we'll see what transpires."

She nodded, but she was still glancing back at Owen, head cocked on one side. It made him smile. She was trying to work out why he was going to see Elwood. She was an intelligent, intuitive woman, and as usual that made him hanker for more of her.

When Owen arrived at Flynn Elwood's office later that morning, he didn't wait to be announced. Bypassing the secretary he opened the door and walked in. Elwood was working at his computer and looked up, surprised.

Owen strode up to his desk and put the note down in front of him. "I received this, this morning. Do you know anything about it?"

Elwood picked up the piece of paper, read it, and all color drained from his face. "Good lord." His fingers went to his collar, which he loosened. "No, I don't know anything about it, and I can't think why this would have been sent to you."

What else would he say? Owen took a seat, somewhat unwillingly. Over the course of the morning he had steadily become more aggrieved about this. "I'm here to help the development ideas. This," he prodded the piece of paper that rested on the desk between them, "just makes me wonder what else is going on here that I have to keep my nose out of."

Flynn Elwood swallowed. "I can see that." He looked every bit as outraged by it as Owen felt, which made Owen take a step back. As far as he was concerned, Flynn Elwood was still under suspicion. However it was pretty obvious he didn't approve of the note.

"Any guesses who sent it?"

Elwood pursed his lips and shook his head.

Owen felt like picking him up by his lapels and giving him a good shake. Something was going on in this man's patch, and yet he appeared to be clueless about it. "You do realize this attitude flies in the face of the Cumbernauld's chain manifesto?"

"Yes, I do. I can only apologize for you having received this, I have no idea why it would happen. It's deeply disturbing."

Owen just about kept a grip on his temper. "I spent some time looking at your booking records this morning before I came up here."

Elwood just stared at him, as if waiting for the axe to fall.

"The figures look good. Alas your profit margins are falling, but you knew that already."

"I've tried to find out what's going on." Elwood pressed two fingers between his eyebrows and glanced down at the piece of paper from the desk. He shifted and put out his hand, as if to draw the evidence to his side of the desk.

Owen frowned. Without hesitation, he reached over and lifted the note, folding it and putting into his pocket. "As I said, I'll be keeping my eyes open, and if I receive any more threatening notes like this, it goes straight to the Board of Directors."

Elwood seemed to age before his eyes. "Is there any way I can prevent that happening?"

"That should be obvious. Find out who sent the bloody thing, and fire them!"

* * * *

Miss Moody looked at the USB Alec was plugging in to Sheila Trent's computer with a dubious expression. "Does Sheila know you're taking a copy of the records?"

Luckily, Sheila Trent wasn't around. Alec had got his USB in there as quickly as possible, taking the opportunity to download the database while the boss-lady was away. "It's standard practice. Like I said yesterday, it's all about ticking boxes. That's what we are here to do."

He gave her a big smile. Had he successfully sidestepped her question? After a moment, she nodded.

"I think I'll try to get us a couple of coffees," Monica suggested, and glanced at Miss Moody. "We've been on our feet all morning already," she explained, "and I could certainly do with one. What about you Alec?"

"That would be great. Thank you." He directed the thanks to Miss Moody, building on Monica's effort to get her out of the room.

When she took the hint and left the two of them in the office, they could still hear her moving around in the kitchen area beyond, filling the kettle and opening cupboard doors. Alec was about say something to Monica when he saw that she was chuckling to herself.

"What?"

"I was thinking about what you said, Miss *Moody*." Her eyes sparkled with humor and it was good to see her that way. She was too serious by far. They knew why now, but it seemed unfair. Sure, her talent was a gift. But she had become isolated by it; that was easy to see. Even though she was a sophisticated attractive woman, there was something almost naive about her at times. Her experience had been so limited. It reminded him of some documentaries seem about gifted kids and how difficult it was for them to make friends. He wondered what her sisters were like. She'd mentioned they were close. He was glad she had them, but it occurred to him that what she really needed was a man she could rely on. Somehow, he didn't think she would agree. There was a fierce independence about her.

For some reason, he had to kiss her. He stepped over to her and cupped her face in his hands, stroking his thumb over her cheeks. She was startled when he did, but melted in a moment. The sound of the kettle whistling from the room beyond made him step away.

"How do you take it?" their hostess asked, from the doorway.

They gave her their orders and when she'd gone, Alec nodded at Monica. He kept a watch on his download completion box, and on the doorway, then glanced at Monica as she began to move around the office, touching the surfaces here and there. It was fascinating to see what she chose to touch. She concentrated on objects she could lift from the desk, drawer handles, the backs of chairs, and the edge of the desk in particular. It was there that she paused and moved her hand around, her eyes half shutting in concentration. Cocking her head on one side, she looked thoughtful then reached for the handle on the desk again before making eye contact with him.

Alec knew she was about to say something when the door to the corridor burst open and a suited man in his mid-twenties entered the room. His staff identity badge poked sideways out of his jacket pocket, but Alec wasn't able to read it. By the looks of him, he had a grievance.

"Oh dear," Monica whispered under her breath.

He glared at Alec. "So, you are this bloke who has swanned in from headquarters?"

"One of them. And you are?" He offered a smile and put out his hand, but this bloke wasn't accepting any of it.

He pointed at Alec rather aggressively and shook his head. "You think you can just come in here and take over. Promotion is my job." He prodded himself in the chest, and rounded his eyes at Alec in what some people would consider a threatening manner.

Alec kept his hand extended for another moment.

"Gerry, don't do this." Monica stepped in. "Alec, this is Gerry Paterson, our in-house promotions and PR manager." She offered Alec a rather weak smile. He could see this was awkward for her. "Gerry, this is Alec Stroud, he is Owen Clifford's assistant. They aren't treading on your patch, they're here to help. Use it wisely while it's available." She tried to put it out there as a pitch, which Alec appreciated.

Gerry Paterson continued to glare at him.

Still his hand hadn't been taken, so Alec withdrew it. He kept his smile friendly, though. "You've got nothing to worry about, Gerry. We're circulating amongst all the hotel staff looking for ways we can help you."

When had lying become so easy? It was the nature of the job, and he often assured himself that he helped people like this to keep their jobs by weeding out the troublemakers. Then again, this bloke could be the one spending money on promotional opportunities that never transpired. Nobody was exempt from scrutiny.

Alec forced his mind back through the staff résumé's he'd studied before they arrived here on this mission. From what he could recall, the promotions guy was fairly new. He'd been in place for about two years after the previous person retired. Straight out of college, full of fresh ideas. Owen had yet to take a closer look at how those ideas panned out though.

"Am I going to lose my job?" Gerry asked. He folded his arms across his chest defensively, his expression tense. "I just bought a flat, I've got a mortgage to meet."

"Not that I know of, so please don't look negatively on our visit." Alec couldn't help wondering if he was the one who had sent the note. He seemed rather hot-headed. "You're on my list of the most important people to meet here, so thank you for coming down. You saved me a task."

"This is awkward," Monica murmured, and she looked quite pale. "I should have introduced you earlier."

Alec put up his hand. "It's not a problem." He looked at Gerry Paterson, who seemed to be calming down somewhat. "How about we grab a coffee in the after-sports café and I'll come back to the accounts side of it later. Does that suit you?"

Gerry nodded. In the background, Miss Moody walked in with a tray of cups.

Alec glanced at the computer screen. The file had downloaded. He reached over and ended the process, withdrawing his USB. Then he turned to Miss Moody and apologized.

"I'm sorry, I'm going to be taking coffee with Mr. Paterson here." He put his hand on Gerry Paterson's shoulder, which seemed to make him slump gratefully. Meanwhile, Miss Moody's mood turned even sourer.

"Fine," she snapped.

Alec glanced at Monica. "Monica, this isn't right. Staff morale seems to be at an all-time low, people thinking the worst. We'll have to do something about that."

When he saw humor flickering in her eyes, he grinned and winked.

Chapter Ten

That afternoon Monica escorted Owen and Alec as they spent time with the reception staff. They set up in one of the small meeting rooms that were available for use of business guests. The reception staff came in one by one and had a relaxed, informal meeting with Owen, while Alec worked on his laptop at a nearby desk. Monica did the introductions, provided refreshments, then sat back and enjoyed watching Owen at work.

His charm was exceptional. Both women and men gravitated to him. That was not surprising. The aim of the meetings seemed to be to find out how inspired they were by the company they worked for and their jobs. With clever questions, he managed to find out how much they enjoyed the buzz of providing good service. That was one of the basic tenets of Cumbernauld's chain. It was a great afternoon, because all the staff that he was able to meet that day loved their jobs, and reflected a really good attitude about working with Cumbernauld's.

Most of all Monica enjoyed the time working with Owen and Alec. Above and beyond their personal relationship, it was fresh and exciting to assist in a new approach to the territory she was so familiar with.

"We ought to dine in Shakespeare's tonight," she suggested when all the staff had gone. It was the silver service restaurant, the top level of dining in the hotel. That lunchtime she'd shot home for some more clothing and she'd brought something a bit more casual to wear out of hours. She didn't want them to think she lived in a business suit.

"That menu looked pretty good," Alec said as he packed up his laptop.

"I prefer to have you with room service," Owen said, most seductively, "but if you insist." His smile was telling.

He'd enjoyed the afternoon. That was good, because he'd seemed a bit tense that morning, like his mission was getting to him.

Had they found what they were looking for yet, she wondered.

"If we go back to my office now, I'll book us a table after I've checked my messages."

It felt good when they followed her suggestion, and she'd begun to enjoy walking around in their company. Basking, that was what she was doing. It surprised her that she'd been able to do that. They had made it happen; they had made it easy for her to slip into something comfortable between business and social with them, once they had understood about her secret.

In the elevator, she took the opportunity to ask Alec how he got on with Gerry Paterson. She'd been curious about it all day.

Alec gave a gentle laugh. "He had me worried for a while there, but he's off the hook. He's keen and he's hot-headed, but he seems to be pretty sound. I went through the work he's done and his plans and I've been able to track everything he's done through the system accordingly." He tapped his laptop. "I don't think he's our culprit."

"Did you get anything from Miss Moody's office?"

"There was something, a bit of a surprise. I don't think it has anything to do with what you're looking for." She glanced at Owen, who was listening avidly.

"Go on," Alec encouraged.

"Jane Mooney has a crush on Sheila Trent." She shook her head. "That was a real surprise."

"Is it reciprocated?" Alec asked.

"No. Sheila knows about it and she uses it to her advantage, but she's not interested."

Alec eyebrows lifted. "No wonder Miss Mooney is Miss Moody."

Monica nodded. "Unrequited love, it explains a lot." She had felt rather uncomfortable about the discovery. There had been a real aura of sadness in the sexual desire she'd experienced around Jane's desk. Longing, and disappointment. "I know it's not what you are looking for," she added.

Owen shook his head. "Anything and everything might be important."

The elevator doors opened and she led them along the corridor to her office.

"What do you think will be the key?" she asked, when they entered her office and the doors closed. "What is that you're looking for?"

"The more we chat with the staff, the more someone is likely to make a slip."

"That's why you came in as an ideas man, because it gives you free range to chat with everyone?"

He nodded and gave her a lazy smile. She thought about the fact that they were alone, the three of them, in her office. The look in his eyes was possessive. It also made her realize that he had been cautious about looking her way that afternoon. As she thought about it, it occurred to her that he was that way with Alec, too. His attention was all theirs when they were alone, but in the workplace he was the consummate professional. She, on the other hand, had been studying him while he worked, and that had kept her libido simmering. His air of command demanded the total attention of everybody he came into contact with. Yet he did it nonchalantly, it wasn't something he projected, it was the essential Owen. People deferred to him readily. At first she had been curious about Alec's easygoing yet submissive way around Owen, both as his PA, and his lover. Now that she was in a similar position herself, she saw that it was instinctive. Being around Owen made her want to submit to him. It made her long to experience his guiding hand.

And the way he was looking at her right at that moment made her even more horny. Behind her, the phone on her desk bleeped. She leaned over a look at it. "I better check my messages."

As she picked up the phone, Owen walked around her office, studying the place. Alec had put his laptop on top of the filing cabinet, and rested on the cabinet on one elbow, watching her as she perched on her desk, legs crossed at the knee. They were prowling, both of them. It took all of her concentration to make notes on the messages left on her phone.

There was one message she didn't particularly want to hear right then. "Oh no, it's Flynn, he wants me to report to him this afternoon." She glanced at her watch. "In ten minutes."

Alec leaned up against the door to the corridor, his hands nonchalantly in his trouser pockets and a suggestive smile on his face. "Probably wants to hear about all the ins and outs of your time with us." He paused and looked her up and down slowly. "You know, all the *juicy* details."

The way he threw that out there, just like that, made her stare at him. Part of her wanted to laugh—the part of her that wasn't already getting hellishly aroused by what he'd said. Then an image of herself sitting in Flynn Elwood's office, mind drifting to sordid images of her tied up in Owen's suite the night before crept into her mind. How the hell would she concentrate?

She put her hand to her throat, attempting to stay level-headed. "You absolute devil. I won't be able to stop thinking about that when I'm in there."

"Why, what are you thinking about?" Owen asked with faux innocence.

"I was thinking about watching you two." She tried to sound chastising, but it wasn't coming out right.

Alec's eyes sparkled with mischief. "That really turned you on, huh?"

"It's turning me on right now, and that's the last thing I need."

"No," Owen responded, "we can't have you going into Flynn Elwood's office all aroused and looking so wanton. He might be interested, and he's had his chance. You're our woman now."

Our woman now. If she hadn't been horny already, that would have done it. The problem was she was in a pretty bad state. Her underwear was damp and the pulse in her groin was thudding erratically. "You've got me in such a state."

"There you go blaming us again," Alec said with a grin.

She sat on the edge of her desk. That only made it worse and she couldn't help grinding her hips.

Owen opened his jacket and rested his hand on his belt. "Anything we can do to help you out?"

"Don't you come near me, please." She gave a disbelieving laugh. "Don't touch me, I'm already in a state and it's getting too hard not to touch you."

"You don't have those lost handcuffs anymore?" Owen glanced at her desk.

Alas, they had gone. She shook ahead. "The owner collected them after I left the office yesterday, security let them in. Besides…I don't do stuff like this. I never have sex in my office!"

"But you have to do something, don t you?" Owen's mouth was locked in a suggestive, sensuous smile. "You can't go in and see Elwood in this state."

"You're supposed to be out there hunting down a finance leak. What would the members of the Board think if they saw you…colluding with a member of staff, trapping her in her office in order to get her aroused?"

Alec shook his head. He appeared to be amused by that. “Oh, I have a feeling the Board would approve of this particular event.”

Owen gave him a sidelong glance then shrugged his shoulders. Monica sensed something pass between them and their barely restrained humor, but Owen quickly pressed on. “We know you, Monica. You’re a good girl. You’ll make up the time. You can always stay after hours, make sure the guests are comfortable in their suites.”

Alec gestured at her hips. “Masturbate, quickly, we won’t tell…so long as you let us watch.”

The suggestion made her face burn. “You’re a devil.”

“You’ve never touched yourself, in the privacy of your office?”

“Maybe. Stuff like those handcuffs…well, you can imagine.” She rolled her eyes.

Both of them looked like they were imagining. The atmosphere in the office intensified, the humor of the moment drifting into something much more specific.

“Do it. Lift up your skirt, so we can see you.” Owen’s tone was commanding. He’d grown serious. He meant it, he really meant it.

“Owen, please.” Her face flamed.

“Monica, lift your skirt up and show us what you’ve got underneath.”

She cursed under her breath. But he was right on one point, there was absolutely no way she could go to a meeting with Flynn in this state, and if either of them—or both of them—touched her, that would only make it worse because she would want more. She had to get relief and quickly. She stood up. With her hands on the sides of her skirt, she slowly eased it up. Both men watched, riveted. She paused when she revealed the black lacy G-string she had on underneath.

Owen folded his arms across his chest, and leaned his shoulders back against the wall. He gestured with one finger. "All the way up, to your waist."

She did as instructed, bunching the fabric at her waist. She felt incredibly rude and shameless, standing in front of the desk in her stacked heels with her skirt hoisted up and two men staring at her. It was empowering though, the way they looked, the commanding tone in Owen's voice and his obvious need to see her.

"You're horny, aren't you?" Owen delivered the comment as if he was remarking on the tidiness of her office.

"You know I am."

"No. I need to be sure exactly how horny you are." His gaze lowered to the front of her underwear. "That scrap of lace that you are wearing…is it damp?"

Alec shifted. "I'd put money on it."

Owen shook his head, and took a slow, obvious intake of breath. "I think we need to know for sure."

The way they were talking about her while she stood there on display made her heart thunder. She was at their beck and call, but she wanted to be. Not knowing what they would ask her to do next was incredibly arousing. It baffled her that she could feel this embarrassed, and yet so aroused that she would have to come before she left the office.

"Take them off." Again Owen gestured with one finger.

When she hesitated, he repeated the instruction.

A sense of shame rushed over her, and she moved awkwardly—still holding her skirt up with her elbows—and eased the band on her G-string down. The fabric clung to her damp groove, and she had to give it a gentle tug. The pull of the fabric on her sensitive, swollen folds made her gasp aloud.

Owen's eyebrows went up. "Oh my, you are wet."

"She might have to go knickerless," Alec commented, "when she rolls up to the boss's office."

Monica cursed under her breath.

She managed to get the G-string to her knees then dropped it. It fell around her ankles.

"Alec, bring the evidence so that I can examine it."

Alec sprang into action. Striding over, he dropped into a squat by her feet. He looked up at her with that now-familiar mischief sparkling in his eyes. "Lift your foot."

She did so, one at a time, and he retrieved the undies. He passed the lace through his hands as he remained at her feet, then stood up and looked deep into her eyes for a moment. He lifted the underwear and dangled it from one finger. Before he turned back to Owen, he winked at her.

Owen took the offering from his hand and held the underwear up to the light.

Humiliation washed over her when she saw the damp patch against the light. He tutted, then he took the fabric to his nose and inhaled. "You have the most enticing aroma."

Swaying on her feet, she pleaded with him silently, desperate for relief.

"Sit on the edge of the desk, and open your legs."

One step back and she was against the desk, and grateful for its support. She lowered her bare buttocks onto the wooden surface. For a moment she couldn't bring herself to open her legs, but Owen shook his head and gave her a disappointed look, and she put her hands on her knees, swinging them apart before she could think about it any longer. With her feet pivoting on her heels and her legs open that way, the cool air did nothing to quell her need for relief. It seemed to make it worse, prickling over her exposed pussy.

"That's quite a sight, don't you agree?"

Alec nodded. "I could look at the view all day long, of course it could get problematic." He rested his hands over the impressively large bulge in his tailored trousers. "And Mr. Elwood is waiting for the lady."

Damn. They kept reminding her of that, which made her want to rush and they were taking their own sweet time with this.

"Do you want to touch yourself?" Owen asked.

"Yes." She hung her head, unable to meet his stare. Between her breasts the skin grew damp and her bra felt far too tight. She longed to fling off the rest of her clothes and lie back on the desk and beg them to fuck her, but there wasn't enough time.

Owen had passed her underwear to Alec and he was squeezing it in his hand, inhaling her scent, and looking at her with hungry eyes.

Owen spoke. "You've been a good girl. I think we'll let you touch yourself."

She pressed her hand tightly against her pussy. A pang of relief shot through her groin, darts of pleasure rising through her, making her entire skin prickle. She shut her eyes for a moment. Then she squeezed and moved her hips back and forth so that her hand pressed against her clit.

"Looks good," Alec commented.

But a moment later she had to pause, and she jerked her hand away. Her eyes flashed opened and she looked at them, stunned. "Damn!"

The carnal energy emanating from her sex was way beyond what it would normally be, and her fingers needled with static, memories of the pair of them licking and sucking her that first night raced through her mind, obscuring her vision. "Damn it, I can't even touch myself anymore, I'm getting feedback."

"Fascinating," Owen stated. "I don't know what to suggest, sweetheart. We can't help you out, there isn't time, remember." That he was enjoying this show was blatantly obvious.

Frustration hit her, and she scanned the desk for something she could use. Her hairbrush sat behind her computer monitor and she snatched it up and quickly pressed the bristles against her pussy.

"Oh Christ, yes," she cried with relief when the stiff bristles stimulated her swollen clit, making it thrum with pleasure.

"Very creative," Owen commented. "Only problem is we need a better view. Can you accommodate us, Ms Evans?"

She lifted one leg, resting one high heel on the handle on a drawer of the filing cabinet. "That better?"

"Much."

She ran the handle of the hairbrush down her slit, then pushed it inside her sex. Her core grasped at the hard intrusion gratefully and she worked it in and out quickly, her gaze riveted on the two men in front of her.

"You are the most incredible woman I have ever met," Owen said in a husky voice as he watched.

That pushed her closer. The handle of the hairbrush was slick with her juices as she worked it in and out ever faster. When she came, a moment later, it was with a disbelieving laugh. Hurriedly, she tried to straighten her clothing. "How in hell am I going to front up to Flynn Elwood after this?"

Alec grinned. "We have every faith you'll manage it."

Owen nodded. "And we'll be waiting for you in my suite, to make sure you passed the test."

"You are dangerous!" She meant it, but strangely enough right at that moment, she loved it.

Chapter Eleven

"Don't let them out of your sight."

It was the last thing Monica expected Flynn Elwood to say, but he looked stressed to the hilt.

"I've been with them pretty much all the time, apart from a couple of hours to make sure my regular duties were seen to."

"Don't worry about your regular duties." Elwood tapped his fingers rapidly on his desk, a sign that he was unhappy about the way things were going. "They refused to be supervised by anyone else. They've spoken very highly of you, Monica. Alec Stroud said that your knowledge of the hotel is unsurpassable, and they wouldn't use anyone else to supervise their time here." He lifted his hand in acknowledgement. "I appreciate all you are doing, but I'm going to have to ask you to keep an even closer watch on them. They have been hiving off into different areas of the hotel, and I want to keep track on what these guys are saying and doing." He looked thoughtful, then continued. "If they have some grand scheme for development, I want to know all about it before it goes to the Board of Directors."

"I can appreciate that." *Some hope*, she thought to herself. She couldn't imagine Owen falling into line with anybody else's demands about how things should be done. Now that she knew he was looking for something specific, she thought he'd been even less likely to share with Flynn.

Flynn tugged at his woolly grey eyebrows. She had only ever seen him do that when his brother died. Her heart went out to him. They had known each other a long time, and in the main he had been a good boss. He'd gained her unconditional loyalty. So what had happened now? It was with a sudden sinking feeling that she realized she worked for the other side, effectively. When it struck her, she felt a little nauseous. She'd never been in this situation before.

"We're all working towards the same goal, at the end of the day, aren't we?" she asked, tentatively. "We all want the success of the hotel, and if they can come up with new ideas and..." *weed out any problems*, "...it's all good, isn't it?"

Flynn looked at her and nodded, but it was with a resigned expression. "The trouble is I'm getting on. They've got me worried that I am losing my touch here. I'm thinking about retirement soon, and I don't want to go out on a downbeat. I've made my mark on this place. I don't need some highflying whiz-kids to coming in here and telling me what I'm doing wrong."

That made her feel even worse.

When she went to leave, Flynn called out after her. "I know you've already been working after hours with these chaps, dining with them and so on. If it makes it easier for you to stay on site, please book yourself into one of the suites."

Again his remark did nothing to ease her conscience. It would make things easier for her, because she wouldn't have to worry about housekeeping staff seeing her in the corridors at all hours. If she accepted his offering, however, it was partly because it made it easier for her to be around Owen and Alec. Was she allied with them now? Was this meeting with her genuine boss a sham? If it was, was she doing it for sex, lured by clever seduction? What did that say about her credibility, and her morals? She was a fiercely loyal employee, and the realization split her in two.

"Thank you. I might take you up on that. We'll see."

As she left his office and thought about the fact she was assisting the henchmen from the Board of Directors to out possible misdemeanors in the running of cash and credit transactions through the books—and her loyalties remained firmly split.

The leisurely silver service in Shakespeare's restaurant was moving a little too slowly for Owen's liking. Room service would have been preferable, but Monica had insisted they try all the restaurants while they were there, stating that they ought to, even if only to uphold their surface 'ideas' mission.

She was rather subdued this evening, and that made him concerned. Something had happened at her meeting with Elwood, which was not surprising after his own encounter with the man that morning. What had been said? Demanding to know would be the wrong thing to do. On the plus side, she had changed out of her business suit, and that indicated a shift in their relationship to his mind. The blue dress she wore was still smart, but more casual than her day attire.

"Is it always this slow?" he asked.

Monica smiled. "It's meant to be an experience."

"I want to get you somewhere more private."

"Have patience." The expression in her eyes warmed.

She still wanted to play, which put one worry to rest. Elwood was bound to have passed on some of his current misery, and Owen hoped that was all it was. He vowed to bring her mood back before the evening was out.

He glanced at Alec. "How are you getting on with that database?"

Alec frowned. "Definitely a few odd adjustments, but I can't quite figure out how they work. I will, in time. Another day or two should do it." He glanced at Monica with a smile. "Unless Monica here can speed things up, with her secret agent super skill."

"What had you in mind?" She seemed pleased to be needed.

Alec shrugged. “I wonder if you thought it might be worth going back to the accounts office, outside hours. You were interrupted, after all.”

“You really think the problem is there, don’t you?” Owen asked. He wanted to see the accounts offices for himself now.

“Just a hunch.”

“I’m willing,” Monica replied. “We could pop up there after dinner, while it’s quiet. I can access the admin floor. I just need to let the security guard know that I am going to be there, beforehand.”

“That sounds good,” Alec stated and gave Owen a meaningful glance. “I did uncover one scam today,” he added, while he swirled and studied the claret in his wine glass.

“Really?” Monica looked startled.

“Something big?” Owen asked.

“Nope.” Alec sipped the wine, before he continued. “One of the doormen has a backhander going with a nearby car valet company. Nothing major.”

“Do you think there may be more going on there?”

Alec pursed his lips and shook his head. “I rattled him when I made it obvious I had noticed, but it’s the usual run-of-the-mill stuff, nothing worth chasing.”

Monica’s jaw fell. “Run-of-the-mill? You mean this sort of thing goes on all the time?”

Alec reached over and nudged her wine glass closer to her. “You’re so adorable when you are shocked, here have a drink.”

She picked up the glass. “I don’t want to drink too much if we’re going up to the accounts office later. I’ll have to speak with security.”

“Good call.”

The food arrived and they had just started to eat when Monica put her cutlery down.

"Oh no." her face paled.

Owen followed her line of vision over to the entrance of the restaurant. Flynn Elwood was on his way over to their table.

"Good evening, gentlemen, Monica." He nodded at each of them in turn. "I heard you were dining here this evening and I thought I'd stop by and say hello before I head home to my lovely lady wife." There was a forced cheerfulness about him that had Owen's radar up.

Monica had one hand on the table—unusually—and rolled a spoon back and forth. She looked as if she wished the earth would swallow her. Had Elwood put her in a difficult position?

"I have advised Monica to use one of the suites and stay on site, so she can be on hand if you need any information urgently."

Owen's attention flared. She hadn't told them that, and she looked sheepish now it was out.

As soon as Flynn left them Monica reached for her wine glass and took a big slug from it, her earlier comment about abstinence apparently forgotten.

Owen reached out and touched her forearm. "You're uncomfortable, that makes me concerned."

"A little, yes. I just feel as if I'm betraying my boss, working so closely and…secretly…with you two, about this fraud thing." She sighed. "I keep telling myself that we're all working for the same goal, the success of hotel."

Owen couldn't completely agree with that analysis, so he didn't respond.

"You shouldn't feel uncomfortable, because ultimately Owen is your boss," Alec offered, "he represents the Board of Directors in this situation."

Owen shot him a sidelong glance. Alec was getting a bit too relaxed around Monica. When he looked back at Monica, he saw that she had picked it up.

He attempted to gloss over it. "And you're right. We are all working for the ultimate success of the hotel…that is everyone except whoever is behind the fraud, that's our job to find out."

Still she stared at him. "What is your job? I mean, what are you? Have you been hired by the Board? Are you private investigators?"

Shit. He'd been hoping this wouldn't crop up.

An awkward silence fell over the table as she stared at them both. Alec opted to reach for his claret. It was his right to leave the question out there, he was a PA. Owen was the one who had to answer it. "No, we're not private investigators."

How he hated to see the insecurity and wariness that developed in those beautiful eyes of hers.

"What, then…?"

"I'm a member of the Board. Well, I'm on trial at the moment." He scrubbed his chin with his knuckles.

Her eyebrows drew together. "I didn't recognize your name as one of the Board members."

"I'm the newest member. I'm Jack Monroe's son." He waited for the reaction, and sure enough it came.

Her eyes rounded. "Oh."

"My legal name is Owen Clifford-Monroe. I'm working under my mother's name so that I keep my connection to the Board of Directors under wraps."

Again she reached for her wine glass. "So I *am* working for you."

Her voice had gone quiet and it felt as if she was pulling away from them. He didn't like that. It might have been easier if she had accused him of keeping information from her, but she didn't, because of course she knew she had no right to.

"I'd appreciate it if you kept that to yourself."

"Of course, I understand." She did, of course she did. She had her own secret to guard.

"You're a sensitive, intelligent woman. I'm the major shareholder's son, and you must understand that kind of information would go against me while I look into this matter."

Her gaze lifted from the half eaten meal on her plate. "Yes, I do understand. It just feels really odd…especially since I am sleeping with you…both."

"That's another issue altogether."

"Hmm." She did a sideways double take.

Her expression was so adorable that he had to quash a chuckle. "I'm sorry, queenie."

Her eyebrows shot up. "Queenie?"

"Ice queenie."

She reached for her claret. "I can see that's going to haunt me forever."

"Only because it's so ludicrous."

She smiled, and one corner of her mouth dimpled.

Somehow he'd managed to level it, for now. But he knew she wasn't as comfortable with them as she had been twenty-four hours before, or even that morning. That got under his skin and stayed there, irritating him, making him want to resolve it. When he glanced over at Alec, he saw that his partner had joined in with the joke, but he was thoughtful too.

Measure your strides, Owen told himself. He didn't want to mess this up, because he wanted her, they both did.

Monica took a deep breath and stepped into the staff elevator. They were headed for the admin offices, and she'd already had to alert security that they were going in there.

"You do realize that by morning everyone will know we accessed the admin offices overnight."

Owen stepped into the space behind her. "Yes, it's a possibility. If it happens, I'll take responsibility."

Once Alec was in, she pressed the button.

"If you don't want to do this," Owen said, "you don't have to."

He seemed so attuned to her moods, there seemed little point in pretending she was finding this easy. "I offered, in good faith. I'll see it through. It just feels a bit odd, you know…out of the ordinary."

The whole thing was out of the ordinary, business and private. She needed some time alone. Time out to absorb all the information that had been put her way. She was confused. What she needed to do was pull back and be more objective, but she was getting more deeply entrenched by the minute. Flynn's appearance at the meal dumped her right in it. She would now have to check into a suite. She should have done so earlier, but she'd been chatting to her sister Faye on the phone. That was necessary because her sisters were the only ones she could really trust. She'd asked them to meet up with her for lunch the following day, because she badly needed their advice. That had leveled her for a while. Their objective take on her strange work situation would help. However, things had become even more complicated since then.

She stared across at Owen. This man who she had come to terms with as a colleague and a lover now turned out to be the son of the major shareholder of the Cumbernauld's chain. That made it feel even more wrong than it had done before. Yet just looking across the elevator at him made her want to drop to her knees and beg him to make love to her. It was hard to regret getting involved, but there were so many reasons why she shouldn't have. Even though she'd told herself over again that she knew it wouldn't last, it felt as if the time was slipping away even faster because she couldn't keep sleeping with him and Alec. Not now.

The elevator doors opened, and she led them along the admin offices to accounts, where she used her master key to open the door. Flicking on the light over the desks, she felt a tad easier about the situation when she heard the door click closed behind them. Alec locked it. Once he'd done so, he came over and massaged her neck and shoulders, his thumbs working magic between her shoulder blades.

"Let's do it," she said a moment later and began to focus.

The two men remained quiet and observant and let her do her thing. She began where she'd felt something that morning, touching Jane's Mooney's desk inquisitively. Again she was flooded with the unfulfilled desire, and images of Sheila.

"Jane Mooney is unhappy in her job, that's for sure." She moved her hands across the desk and down the front of the drawers in the unit beneath. As she touched a handle on one drawer, she felt something else, and images flashed through her mind. The way Sheila talked to Jane when no one was around surprised her. "Oh!"

"What is it?"

"She's really browbeaten by Sheila and that makes her unhappy." She moved her fingers around the drawer handle and felt the frustration in Jane. A moment later she nodded and broke contact. When Jane was unhappy, she went for sweet treats that she kept in a drawer. That clashed with her concerns about fitness and remaining slim. The results were not pretty. She would never have guessed that Jane was bulimic.

It wasn't anything that her companions would be interested in, but it made her feel even more uncomfortable about what she was doing. It was too close for comfort, reading the experience and emotions of a colleague. It was one of the things that she was very careful not to do. “This is the sort of thing that is going to make my job difficult. She’s rather fatally attracted to Sheila. I never knew it.”

“And you don’t think they’re involved?” Alec asked.

“From what I can see Sheila plays on it, demanding Jane’s loyalty. It’s not very pleasant.” She couldn’t keep the distaste from her tone. She pressed on, moving to the mouse on the computer then the mouse mat. Concentrating, reaching past the sexual energy, she sought for clues. Eventually, a wisp of an image floated through her mind, and Jane’s emotions with it. “This might be more relevant. Jane found something that wasn’t right in the books. I’m sure of it.”

She pulled her hands free, unwilling to commit herself if she wasn’t sure. Most of all it was the heavy and pressing sense of guilt that had built over the course of the evening taking her over. Ever since her meeting with Flynn it had got a grip. She wanted to help Owen and Alec, but the guilt made her drag her feet. Her heart wasn’t in it, and she felt bloody awful doing this.

She stood up, restless and uneasy. “I’m sorry. This is making me uncomfortable.”

“Then stop it, right now.” Owen moved closer and put his hands on her hips.

The way he was—so gorgeous, so powerful and commanding—she would do anything for him. But she still didn’t feel right about it, because she felt she was betraying so many of the things that she had put her faith in, things that had been her anchors for years. There was no doubting the fact that she had to pull free from the situation and gather her thoughts. She’d become vulnerable. Too much had been said, and she knew that there was pressure on both sides. It was getting to her, and she couldn’t tell if she was being manipulated and, if so, who or by what?

Desire, most of all, is what it is, she thought with irony as she glanced from Owen to Alec and back again.

"Hey." His hands moved quickly and he stroked her upper arms.

He'd sensed her turmoil. That made her ache.

"This feels good."

She nodded and glanced away to Alec, his long-term lover. Instinctively, she reached out for him, and he touched the back of her hand. That made her melt. They remembered her boundaries more than she did. *That's because I'm losing control.*

Owen looked deep into her eyes. "Are you okay?"

No, I'm not. "I'm confused."

It was the understatement of the century but it was enough.

Concern spilled from him. "I'm sorry, we shouldn't have let you do this, it was wrong and I—"

Instinct led her and she put her fingers to his lips, interrupting him. When she did and her fingers made contact with his mouth, it affected her deeply.

"Oh, I shouldn't have done that." She went to pull her hand away, but he wouldn't let her. He held her hand there and kissed her fingertip before he let it go.

The rush of sexual energy that hit her made her ripple and sway, and she latched her hands behind his neck. Before she could say another word, he was kissing her. With his arms locked around her back he drew her closer, and pushed away the moral obstacles standing between them.

God help me I want this man so badly. All of it. I want everything he might bring, including Alec.

When he drew back, he eased her towards the desk, trapping her between him and it. "You saw something when you touched my mouth. What did you see?"

He was asking because it had turned her on. "I saw myself…I saw you, making me come."

His eyes glowed with certainty, as if he made some discovery and he was pleased by it. “Crazy as it sounds, and hard though it is for you, I love that you saw that.”

Oh, how that primed her for sex, sending her pulse wild.

Alec walked around them, observing. “There is a certain fascination about it.”

He reached in and stroked her cheek, tenderly, then strolled on.

“Nothing that frightened you off?” Owen asked.

“No. It was brief, and…” She felt for the edge of the desk with her hands, the urge to have his body over hers taking her over. “…incredibly hot.”

When she rested back on her elbows, Owen moved on it. He pushed up her skirt until it was bunched at the top of her thighs. “Hot, hmm?”

She nodded.

He put the back of his hand to her underwear, rocking his knuckles from side to side against the swell of her pussy. “Well, I can confirm that the heat coming off you is immense.”

She laughed softly, the pressure of their work situation fading away for a few moments while she allowed herself to fall totally under his spell and his attention was so fully hers. “You started it.”

He kissed her again while he pushed her knees apart to stand in between them. She clasped her hands round his neck, unwilling to let go. She knew she would have to do just that, soon, but right now her body craved more of what it was getting. *Quickly, here and now, then break with them tomorrow. One last night of adventure*.

“Still confused?” he whispered as he moved down to kiss her in the dip of her cleavage.

“Like you wouldn’t believe.” She lifted her hands away from him, closing her fingers into her palms as she rested them on the desk above her head. "One thing I am sure of, I need you now. Quickly Owen, please, before I change my mind." The knowledge that she was going to break with them made her desire soar, lust taking control of her.

He rested his hands on the desk either side of her chest and looked deep into her eyes. Silence stretched, and she thought he was going to refuse her.

"Alec, take control of Monica's hands," he instructed without breaking eye contact with her.

The urgency she felt was reflected in him too, and her breath caught in her throat when he grappled for her hips and quickly found the band on her underwear, hauling the barrier down.

Alec had moved to the opposite side of the desk and gripped both her wrists in his hands, pinning her down. "Thank you," she whispered.

"Hush." He kissed her right at the corner of her mouth.

Her hips rolled when Owen tore off her underwear. He went for his belt then the zipper. The sound of the zipper opening ran ragged over her nerve endings. He reached into his pocket and pulled out a condom packet. Then he had his cock in his hand and was rolling the rubber onto it.

Sheer lust had taken over. Wantonly, she undulated against the hard surface of the desk, her head rolling from side to side.

Owen put his hands around her hips and hauled her closer, positioning her bottom right on the edge of the desk. Her arms were at full stretch and Alec leaned over her so that he could hold her wrists with one hand. With his free hand he reached over to her shirt and popped open two buttons so that he could reach inside and touch her breasts. She was limp as a rag doll, the nagging ache at her centre controlling her every thought, her body desperate for what they could give her.

Owen positioned his cock at her opening and moved it there, as if testing her. He shook his head. "Christ, you're wet."

She nodded and her hips had began to roll, inviting him in. Owen watched her a moment longer then he lifted her legs and drew them over his shoulders. That way, when he did thrust in he went really deep, and she cried out.

"Alec, silence her," Owen said from between gritted teeth. "Security will be down here and we can't have the lovely housekeeping manager being caught *in flagrante delicto* on the accountant's desk now can we?"

He grinned, and she looked at him in his designer suit and his white shirt, with her legs over his shoulders and his cock buried inside her—here, on the accountants desk—and all the guilt and longing and regret and desire bunched in her chest, making her anxious.

He eased out, only to slam back in, making her buck.

Alec, meanwhile, had moved around to the side of the desk. He took his hand from her mouth and silenced her with his kiss instead, his hand back inside her shirt, fingers inside her bra tweaking her peaked nipple. The thrust of his tongue into her mouth and the thrust of Owen's cock inside made her crazy for it. She heard her skirt rip, but didn't care. Her legs were bent double and Owen thrust into her hard and fast, so deliberately rough that she could feel the desk vibrate.

"You're determined to bring the security down here, aren't you," she accused breathlessly when Alec came up for air.

"No," Owen responded, "I just love the way you feel and once I get started…"

The squeak of the desk legs against the floor made her bow against him, resisting his thrusts, yet inviting him deeper. Her chest knotted when the blunt head of his cock thrust up against her centre. "Oh!"

"Oh, yes." His cock turned to steel, then jerked in release.

Her core clamped on him. She turned her face away but met Alec's mouth. Her womb buoyed up then release barreled through her. Her muted cry let loose in Alec's mouth.

This moment would stay with her forever.

Tomorrow, it'll be over.

Chapter Twelve

Monica got out of their bed next morning and concentrated on the act of getting dressed for the day.

"Aren't you staying for breakfast?" Owen asked, rising from the bed.

He was blatantly aware of her mood. Overnight he'd held her close against him as if he knew she was going to break from them.

"I've got a bunch of stuff I have to do before I can make myself available to you today. And I have a lunch meeting. It's a family thing that I can't get out of." It came out like a business comment, but she couldn't help that. She was retreating into her shell. Once she'd had that discussion with her sisters and put everything into perspective, she would tell him that she couldn't carry on their affair.

Owen was about to reply when there was a knock at the door. He frowned at it. Before he had a chance to get to it, it opened.

"Oh no." Monica stared at the intruder and her heart sank. It was one of her own housekeeping staff.

Linda stared at them with a look of astonishment on her face. Monica burned up. Owen was completely naked. It didn't matter that she was fully dressed, the implication was more than obvious.

"I'm so sorry," Linda said, hurriedly, and then backed out of the room.

"That's all I need." Monica grabbed her bag and threw him a regretful glance.

"You might have just arrived," Owen offered.

Monica gave a soft laugh at the comment, and glanced at his naked body, regret and anxiety filling her. "Discretion is part of a housekeeper's duty, and Linda is reliable. I've never known her to gossip, but I still can't guarantee it."

Owen took her in his arms, and kissed her forehead. "I know that is important to you. You are important to me. Increasingly so."

Doubts crowded in on her. *Important, why?* Because she was convenient, and useful? The more he held her like this, the more difficult it was going to be. She knew that she should talk to Flynn and ask to be relieved of her duty to escort them. One thing was for sure, she needed her support network. She needed her sisters.

"I've put my phone number in your phone," he said, "under my name. Call me when you're done with your duties."

Monica couldn't even bring herself to look at him. Instead she nodded, then turned away.

Owen's mood nosedived. Tension had built overnight. The evening before she'd wanted them both, and had made love to them both, but there was resignation and sadness in her and it bugged the hell out of him.

After she'd gone he distracted himself for a while by making calls. He talked to his father and alerted him to the fact they were getting closer. Then he grabbed cold coffee from the breakfast tray he'd ordered, showered and dressed. Once he'd done that, he found Alec busy on his laptop in the sitting-room.

When he went to join him, he saw that there was another note on the carpet by the door. "Oh, great."

He ducked down and scooped it up.

"Our friendly neighborhood psycho thief?" Alec asked.

"Yes." He'd been hoping that it was some kind of in-house pamphlet, but it was the same scrawled capital letters on a piece of printer paper. He shook his head as he read it.

We know that you're fucking the housekeeping manager, Mr. Clifford.

If you do not want the information to be passed to headquarters, leave now.

"Who the bloody hell has sent this?"

Alec looked at it over his shoulder. "What about housekeeping? You said someone came in this morning."

"Monica thought she was sound. Of course Monica thinks everyone is as professional as she is, to a fault. All it would take is for the housekeeper to have whispered it to one buddy, for it to get passed around. Doesn't mean it was anyone in housekeeping who sent this."

Sometimes, that was the trouble with the hotel trade. Gossip amongst the staff passed around like wildfire. They were looking for stuff that would break the routine, and this would be a juicy piece of gossip. Especially if Monica hadn't had any relationships here before. Monica would be upset by it. That was the killer. She had an unrealistically pure view of the working world that sadly wasn't the case. He didn't want to be the one to break it to her, but she would be better off knowing that there were unscrupulous people in all walks of life.

The situation was screwing with his head. He was almost ready to walk out on his job here, because Monica was unhappy. One glance at Alec assured him that he was uneasy too. They'd shared women before and they worked well as a team. Up until now, however, the women had wanted all the attention for themselves. With Monica, she was into their relationship too. It turned her on, and that kind of balance was the Holy Grail as far as he was concerned.

"What the hell am I going to do? I can't just ignore it."

Alec gave a wry smile. "Of course you can. What you have to ask yourself is how likely to pull a prank like that are they, if they are involved in illegal activities? And, if they are loopy enough to do that, does it even matter to you?" Alec gave him that look, the one that drilled way deep in his soul.

Owen gave a wry smile. "What would I do without you? You're right. It's safety I'm concerned with, not reputation. I'm not a married man, she's not a married woman. As long as you're okay with me having a relationship with Monica, that's all I care about."

Alec smiled and his eyes twinkled mischievously. "In that case ignore it."

"Agreed. We do need to tell Monica about this though."

"We can do that tonight when we get back here," Alec responded. "You do realize she could probably tell us who sent it, just by holding it?"

Owen gave a quiet laugh as he processed that information. "Christ, you're right." They looked at each other for a long moment, silently sharing the depth of how they felt about her. "She's an amazing woman," Owen eventually added, because he felt humbled by everything she was.

Being with her sisters made Monica feel so much better. The familiar activity and the understanding company grounded the contrary and disturbing emotions that held her captive, if only for the duration of their time together.

Once a fortnight the Evans' sisters convened for lunch, midweek. Monica had requested they bring the meeting forward because she needed to talk. They met at their favorite Italian coffee house, Luigi's. It was just a short walk from the hotel, and they got the most delicious toasted paninis there, and coffee that even Monica admitted rivaled Cumbernauld's best.

She smiled across the table at her sisters. Faye looked fine, if a little concerned about her siblings. Holly looked dreadful. Her face was paler than ever and a perma-frown was etched between her eyebrows.

Monica reached out and covered Holly's hand with the back of her own. "You look tired."

Holly nodded. "It's this thing that's happened with my neighbor. Since the accident he was involved in I can't sleep at night, not for long, not when he's awake." Her eyes flashed closed. "It's the weirdest thing."

Monica exchanged knowing glances with Faye. Emotion and arousal had sprung from Holly as she closed her eyes, and they'd both felt it. There was something meaningful between her and this neighbor. Faye mimed a beating heart. Monica hushed her with a hand gesture, but nodded.

"So are you saying you sleep when he sleeps, and wake up when he does?" Faye's delicately arched eyebrows were drawn together as she tried to get her head around it.

Holly sighed. "Yup. I was there just after he was knocked over. I kept him conscious until the ambulance came and since then it's like my psyche is wired to his."

Faye drummed her silver lacquered nails on the table top. "Hmm. It reminds of that eastern belief that when you save someone's life you become responsible for it."

"Oh god, please no," Holly replied. "I can't be responsible for him, please no."

Holly was quite obviously attracted to this neighbor of hers, but she'd barely processed that information herself and she definitely wasn't ready to talk about it yet.

A moment later the waiter arrived with their coffees.

Holly looked grateful. She pushed back her thick blonde hair, automatically plaiting it over one shoulder as she chatted. It was waist length and she obviously hadn't had time to sort it before their meeting. "Sorry, this isn't supposed to be about me." With effort, she smiled. "You asked for the meeting, Monica, please talk. It'll do me good to think about someone else's problems, besides…Joshua."

Monica nodded. "If you need us, just say. Whenever you want to chat."

So, his name was Joshua. Again Monica exchanged glances with Faye. She was willing to bet they would soon be hearing more about this Joshua bloke.

Faye took a sip of her coffee, sat back in her chair and peered at Monica. "Come on, spill. How did your date go?"

"You had a date?" Holly asked, eyes rounded, her own problems temporarily shelved.

Monica tried not to bristle, but she couldn't keep the sarcasm from her reply. "Yes, I had a date, and yes I know it's about time and no I'm not about to turn into a grey-haired spinster." She ran her fingers along the edge of the table then snapped them away when she opened up residual memories of erotic conversations that had gone on here in the past. "To cut a long story short, the date I had was with two guys."

"I knew it," Faye interjected. She grinned. It made her look even more elfin than usual. With her short cropped hair dyed vibrant blue-black and her clothes and make up influenced by her art school days, their Dad had nicknamed Faye the mad pixie of the family.

"You sensed there were two men, yes. But what you didn't know was that they actually came as a pair."

Faye's expression altered into one of wonder. "How does that work?"

Monica fanned herself as she thought back on it. "They're bisexual."

"Oh, right." Faye's lips pursed as she thought it through. "Are you saying that you had a threesome?"

Monica adjusted her collar then leaned over the table. “Keep your voice down, please. Yes, I had a threesome. That’s not what I wanted to talk about, that bit worked out fabulously.”

“Ooh, hark at you.” Faye was in the mood to tease. “Suddenly you’ve gone from no men to two at the same time, and it worked out ‘fabulously’?”

She had a point. A disbelieving laugh escaped Monica. “I know, ludicrous isn’t it?”

It *had* worked out fabulously, that was the truth. It had been way beyond good. It had been steaming hot, and most important of all it had worked for her, really well. Never before had she been able to let go and have an orgasm and she’d had more than one.

Holly was observing with curiosity. “Maybe that’s it —you needed two men because of your psychic ability.”

Monica thought about that, and nodded. It was a good part of it, and there was the bondage angle too, but she wasn’t ready to talk about that as yet. “The problem is I’m working with these guys, and now I feel muddled. It’s like I’m not sure of their motives.”

Her gaze dropped. She was going to have to confess to her sisters that she had told Owen and Alec about her psychometric ability. It was a secret the three of them had sworn to. Monica’s gift made her the most vulnerable. Her talent could be used, as she was all too quickly discovering. If anyone else had to be told, she was supposed to confer with them first.

“Motives?” It was Holly who asked, and Monica noticed that her color was getting better now that she was focused on someone else’s problem rather than her own.

“Look, I hate to admit it, but I told them what I can do. I had to.”

A flicker of disapproval crossed Holly's face, but Monica saw none in Faye's. She was the most chilled of them all.

Faye shrugged. "You must have had to, right?"

Monica nodded.

"Has it put you in danger?"

"I don't think so, not like we thought it might, at any rate. It is complicated though. They are investigating fraud at the hotel, and when we got involved Owen knew I was hiding something. I had to reveal that it wasn't anything to do with the investigation. As it turned out, the set up with the two of them meant I could, well…let go a bit and enjoy it, and you know…without the flood of information crowding me."

"So let me get this straight," Faye said, with humor sparkling in her eyes, "you finally had a good orgasm, but these two men think you're behind fraud in the hotel?"

"They know I'm not, now." Monica couldn't keep the tension from her voice.

"It figures," Faye added, "that it would take two men to handle you, sexually."

"It's not funny," Monica responded.

"I wasn't being funny, I meant it."

That and the bondage, yes. Even as she thought about it, her body yearned for more of the same. "The thing is now that they know what I can do, they want me to help them with their task. And I can't decide whether that's why they want to be with me."

"You want it to be for another reason?" Faye was so sharp, so intuitive. "You like these guys, I can tell."

"I do. What if they walk away and I never see them again?"

Faye reached for her cup, turning it in its saucer. "If they walk away, you had fun, you let go for a while. Don't regret it when it's not even over yet, just enjoy."

Monica looked at Holly. "What say you?"

Holly was more serious. "I say you are afraid of being hurt. I can understand that."

Holly's expression was too knowing. There was a raw nerve there as well.

Monica covered her eyes with her hands for a moment, because something in her chest had knotted. She felt ashamed of the way she had let this thing get away from her so quickly. She wanted them, yes, and her emotions were now tangled up in this. "It's just because I've never been able to let go, not the way I can with them, that's all it is."

Their paninis arrived. Normally the chargrilled vegetables and goat's chèvre would have her mouth watering. The food did look and smell delicious but Monica's appetite was gone.

"That sounded like an excuse," Holly commented as she picked up her panini. "You've fallen for them, haven't you?"

Monica stared at the table. Eventually, she nodded. "Maybe."

Her sisters knew it, and deep down she knew it too.

She had to pull back and quickly, or she would get badly hurt.

An hour later Monica was back at Cumbernauld's. When she got there she went straight to Flynn Elwood's office in order to request someone else take over the duty of being the go-to person for Owen and Alec. It wasn't an easy decision to make, but she knew it was the right thing to do if she was to maintain the necessary structure, boundaries and routine that she needed in her life—in order to survive.

Arabella flicked through Flynn's paper diary. In that respect—as in many others—he was old fashioned, and the paper dairy was the place to look. "He should be here in the office." Arabella glanced up at her. "If it's important you can wait."

"It's important." Monica paced up and down, one hand on her hip the other plucking at the buttons on her jacket.

"Is it anything I can help with?" Whether it was curiosity or concern, Arabella looked genuine.

"Thank you, but I don't think you can. It's a permission thing."

Arabella stepped out from behind his desk. "Okay. Go in and take a seat. I'm going to go pick up some lunch in a minute but I'm sure he'll turn up before long."

Monica took the seat, but once Arabella had gone she fidgeted restlessly then got up and paced about again. She ran over her thoughts, ordering them into a statement. *I hate to be unprofessional, but I'm going to have to ask to be relieved of my obligation to liaise with the bods from HQ.*

She pressed her fingers to her temples. Once she'd made the decision, back there at the coffeehouse, she'd started retreating, internally. It was about self-protection. She was in too deep, and their motivation was completely different to hers. They'd all gone in to it on level ground, for the thrill, for the good sex. That was fair enough. But now her emotions had been involved—she was in danger of being hurt, while they would be able to walk away. *It already hurts. Oh god, I'll miss them so much.*

Apart from anything else, they had each other. They probably seduced a woman everywhere they went, for fun. The whole thing had been a mistake for her, of course it had. For her it had stimulated impossible dreams. How in the hell could she even think about a relationship with men like that? Her secret skill was a barrier to deep commitment, and it always would be. Some people would give their right arm for what she could experience. How ironic. One way or another it had ruined her life. Much more of this and she would grow bitter, and that's what she had tried to avoid by being independent, by being alone. Taking on two men, lovers, was at complete cross-purposes with the basic rules she'd established for her life.

As she thought it through, her emotional state grew acute. Every time she heard voices passing in the corridor she attempted to ready herself to speak with Flynn, but he didn't appear. Where was he anyway? It wasn't going to be an easy meeting. He'd be annoyed that she was dumping them back at his door.

What would he think about the fraud angle, if she mentioned that?

Without full consciousness, she picked up a paperweight from his desk, a glass globe with a flat bottom. Inside was a miniature of the hotel. Peering at it with unseeing eyes—her thoughts far away—she swore aloud when the glass globe warmed in her hands and began to pump images into her mind, fast and furious. Aghast, Monica's breath caught as a scenario opened in her mind.

The globe had been sitting on the desk and it had been nudged over by two bodies entwined—two people having sex. It was Flynn, and a woman. Monica held the globe a moment longer, and she saw the red hair and she knew that it was Sheila Trent.

Flynn and Sheila had an affair.

Quickly, she put the object down and stepped away.

Her mind raced. Alec thought that there was something amiss in the accounts department. She'd figured he was leaning towards Jane Mooney as the culprit, but this shone a different light on things. She paced up and down. What the hell would she say to Flynn, now? If he walked in right at that moment she feared she would be speechless. It was time to make a hasty retreat.

She headed towards the door but when she got to it, she heard a voice outside. With one ear against the door, she quickly realized it was Sheila, and by the sounds of it Flynn was with her.

Bloody hell, I'm trapped in here. She glanced around the room. There was another door. It led on to a closed meeting room, a small boardroom where Flynn gathered the management staff once a month. There was no way in or out of it other than through his office, but if she was lucky she could hide out in there until they were gone.

She darted into that room, pushing the door shut behind her. It was just in the nick of time by the sounds of it. Sheila and Flynn her entered his office. Monica stood behind the door with her heart hammering, unable to risk pushing it completely shut.

Sheila and Flynn commenced a heated discussion, and at first they made some attempt to hush their voices. Monica strained to hear, and when she did she was astonished.

"Why in hell did you do it?" Flynn demanded. "I had that Clifford bloke in here threatening me with the Board of Directors, because you sent that note."

That puzzled her. Owen had received a note and hadn't told her? Then Sheila responded, and Monica's level of astonishment rose.

"Because the longer they look at my accounting system, the bigger the problem."

"Why is that, Sheila?" Flynn replied tersely. "You know that I have been going through hell trying to work out why profits are down, and you kept reassuring me that everything was fine."

"That's because I care about you, more fool me!" Sheila sounded incredibly bitter.

Monica wrapped her hand around the back of her neck. The skin there was damp. She felt physically sick, because her whole world was falling apart. Cumbernauld's was her life, her safe place. *Not anymore*.

She wanted to be out of there. She wanted to be a long way away, where she could slowly pull herself together. There was no way out of the room she was in, but she had got to the point where she had to be done with it, even if it meant saying goodbye to her lovers. If only she could reach Owen. That's when she recalled that he had put his telephone number on her phone. She crept further away from the door, and unclipped her phone from her belt. A moment later she had scrawled to his name. Quickly she sent him a text message:

Flynn's office. Now!

How long would it take him to get there? As she fumbled to get the phone back on her waistband clip, the phone bleeped. Monica stared down at it in horror. On the screen a message stated that the memory was full and her sent message couldn't be saved.

"What was that?" It was Flynn's voice.

Bloody hell. Quickly, she skirted the table and darted to the far end of the room.

A moment later the door sprang open and Sheila Trent stood there. "What the hell are you doing in here?" Her cheeks flushed, her eyes narrowing. "How much did you hear?"

Flynn was behind her and he grimaced as he realized it was Monica was in there.

A sudden sense of clarity came over her. After all that had happened Monica felt a steely sense of calm, because she was angry. She wanted her boundaries back. As she looked at Sheila, she knew that she had three options. She could deny she'd heard anything, she could attempt to leave, or she could confront them.

With a deep breath, she gave her response. "I heard it all, but they are already on to you, Sheila. Something is wrong with the accounting system isn't it? Something you knew about and you are trying to cover up."

Sheila looked even more annoyed, and closed on her quickly.

"Shut your mouth, you silly bitch." She delivered a sound slap to Monica's face.

Astonished, Monica staggered then straightened her spine, one hand going to her cheek to stem the sting. "Exactly what I'd expect from a bully!"

Sheila didn't like that.

Monica built on it. "I know how you treated Jane. It's all going to come out now."

For a moment she regretted saying that, because Sheila looked absolutely furious. Her hands fisted and Monica had the awful feeling she was going to be punched. Mercifully, there was shouting in the office beyond and Arabella and Owen walked into the room.

Immediately—and as per usual—Owen took charge.

The sense of relief Monica felt was so great that she had to bite her lip to stop from laughing when he took over with his customary ease.

"Oh, this is good…this is nice. This works for me." He glanced around at the three of them. "Everybody in one place that I want to speak to this afternoon, I couldn't be happier." He didn't sound happy, he sounded angry, but he also sounded focused. Monica noticed that his tie was half undone and his hair a mess, as if he'd been stressed or rushing.

Sheila went to push past Owen.

Owen blocked her path and pushed her back into the room. "Oh no, you're the star guest, Sheila. We've been looking into your database and we know that you've been creaming off some of the profits for yourself, haven't you?"

Sheila stared at him in silence, shocked.

"Oh, didn't your loyal assistant tell you that we made a copy of your system? Maybe you should have been nicer to her and she would have informed you of that." He glanced quickly at Monica.

Flynn had stood by, as if in shock, and he mustered a plea. "I only found out about this today. The note…"

"You don't know what I've had to put up with," Sheila snapped, viciously. "Years ago he promised he would leave his wife for me, but he's too much of a gutless wonder to do it. If I have to spend my retirement years alone, he's going to pay for it."

"I'm sorry," Flynn said, directing his comment at Owen. "I will present myself to the Board and explain the situation."

"In this situation I would be grateful if you consider me the Board. Jack Monroe is my father."

Flynn staggered then reached for a nearby chair and slumped on to it, elbows on his knees and head in hands. Monica realized that he must have been clinging to the one last hope that he could talk Owen round and present a good case. That chance had gone.

Alec had arrived, with his laptop under his arm. When he saw the gathering, he flicked open his phone and began to make calls.

"As for you, madam," Owen said to Sheila, "the police will need a statement from you."

"No!" Sheila wailed. She broke down in violent tears, gulping for air, and had to be seated and brought a glass of water.

It was then that Monica took her chance to flit past the gathering and out of the door.

She made it through Flynn's office, through Arabella's office, and out into the corridor, but she didn't make it much further down the corridor before Owen was on her heels.

"Monica, where are you going?"

She turned to face him. "It's over now."

When he noticed the mark on her face, rage flitted through his expression. "Did that bastard hit you?"

"No. Sheila slapped me when I confronted her. It's okay."

He ran his thumb around the edge of the mark on her cheek, tenderly.

She wavered and had to pull it together quick or be lost under his touch. "Your work is done and you will soon be gone. Goodbye, Owen."

Disbelief marred his expression. "Goodbye? You can't mean that."

She went to turn away but he grabbed her wrist. "It's not over, we're not over." His expression looked wild. "How can you think that?"

Monica shook her head. Beyond him, she saw that Alec stood in the doorway to Arabella's office, gripping onto the frame with one hand, his free hand on his hip as he watched them with concern. He would be there for Owen. Alec would always be there. Emotion welled inside her, threatening to leave her as much a wreck as Sheila currently was. There was nothing she wanted more than to walk into his arms and accept his comfort, but for what—one more night before they were gone?

She stared up at him and shook her head. "I need my boundaries, and now they are gone. I trusted these people. That has been destroyed."

"I'm sorry."

"It had to be done. It's not your fault, but I need to make *myself* strong again." She put her fist to her chest, swallowing down the emotion.

Her world had been taken apart, everything that was solid and sure that she could build her days around without fear or discovery had turned out to be feeble in the face of a brief affair with two men who would be gone soon. How would she cope when that happened? She needed to rebuild her walls, find the way and make her routine solid again. What she didn't need was raw emotions and the fear of being hurt even more. "Let me go."

She could see the strength of his will in his eyes. They were black, denying what she was saying. But he clenched his lips together, and released her.

"I'll let you go…for now." That sounded like a warning.

Monica moved, turning away.

I have to pull back, before I spin out of control.

Chapter Thirteen

Monica had said goodbye and walked away. Alec was astonished that Owen had let her do that.

The police arrived a moment later. Things were taken out of their control, discussions and procedures demanded their full attention. Later, once he saw Owen leave, Alec made his excuses and headed back to the suite.

By the time Alec got there Owen was packing.

Alec couldn't handle it. Just lately he'd thought Owen and him would go on forever, but not now, not if he was willing to walk away from Monica that easily. His heart thumped against the wall of his chest, his mouth going dry. "You can't just leave!"

"I can. Our work here is done."

Shocked, Alec stared at him. "You can't just walk away from Monica, she's too special."

Owen stopped what he was doing. "I'm not walking away. I'm merely getting ready to leave. We're going home. We're taking her home." He walked over to Alec and put his hand on Alec's shoulder. "She needed time."

Alec felt something inside him buckle. "Right, okay." He pushed his hand through his hair. When Owen smiled at him as if amused by his emotional state, he grinned. "I'm sorry, I lost it."

"I forgive you. Just don't do it again." Owen winked. "Now let's finish up here quickly. We've got to be ready to catch the lady when she makes her move."

"You don't think she's gone already?"

"No. She's in mourning for this place." Owen took off his tie and reached into the wardrobe for his leather jacket, which he shucked on. "We're going to have to break her connection with this branch, don't you think?"

It took a moment for Alec to get the gist of Owen's thoughts, but when he did he nodded quickly. "Absolutely!"

Monica grabbed her coat and bag from her office and located a vacant guest room. Not one of the suites, just a regular room where she could stay away from everyone without the fear of anyone banging on the office door. When she put her phone on the bedside table, she double checked it was on silent then saw that Owen had already sent a couple of text messages. She wanted to read them, but she knew she needed some time alone. She would go home to her flat when all the furor had died down and she didn't have to speak to anyone. That's when she would read them.

There in the anonymous hotel space, she lay on the bed with her hands carefully folded over her waist, and closed her eyes.

Eventually, she dozed.

Strange images assailed her in odd, disjointed dreams. She found herself at the door of the suite where the handcuffs had been found, staring at the door handle and afraid to touch it—afraid to experience whatever mysteries and pleasures awaited her inside.

When she jerked awake, it was with a feeling of loss.

She sat up on the bed and sighed. She'd expected to feel sad that it was over and her secret lovers moved on, their job here done. What she didn't expect was to be left with her former structured and safe world in ruins, or as good as.

Sleet and rain lashed at the window, drawing her attention. It was late, nearly ten. It was time to go home. With resignation, she slid on her shoes and collected her things. Before she left the room she logged in and made a note on the electronic staff calendar for housekeeping to come in and make over the room in the morning. She opted for the stairs and when she pulled on her raincoat she tied the belt tightly and put her collar up. In an effort to go unrecognized as she walked through reception she also let her hair down.

Luckily, the reception area was busy. A coach load of Italian guests had just arrived and were checking in. The large expanse of black and white marble floor was littered with suitcases. As she made her way across the space, she glanced at the open fireplace on her left, where a roaring fire welcomed the guests to London. The myriad of lamps around the place and low, comfortable armchairs were so familiar, and yet she felt she was looking at it all with a new perspective. Distance, even. Nothing had been what it seemed. She'd come here every day thinking that her job and the hotel was her safe place. She couldn't have been more wrong. Integrity was no longer the key to success here, as she had been told when she joined the company. Her trust had been misplaced, and it appeared that she'd been oblivious of the real story.

As she stepped through the sliding glass door, the icy cold air outside hit her. It felt fresh and exhilarating. Perhaps some time away from Cumbernauld's would be a good idea. She pulled her collar higher. Moments later, she sidestepped the doorman then hurried down the steps and away from the awnings over the entrance to the hotel, before darting away into the rainy night.

She'd scarcely got twenty paces when Owen stepped out in front of her.

"Monica, we have to talk." He wore a leather jacket, collar up. Rain glistened on his shoulders and his hair was stuck to his head. The sight of him waiting for her in the night affected her strangely. She noticed how handsome he was, how intense. Determined, too. He'd been waiting in the sleet and rain. For her. She glanced past him, but there was no sign of Alec.

"I can't, not right now, I need…space." Even as she said it, it felt like a lie. What she needed was to be in his arms. She was reeling herself in, trying to make everything right in her world, because this couldn't last. The secret that she lived with meant it was impossible for her to have a normal relationship. The longer she tried to do that, the harder it would get.

And yet here he was.

He didn't say anything, which unnerved her. Instead he studied her intently.

How long had he been waiting out here for her? For a moment she thought she couldn't force herself to turn away, but she made herself to step to one side to get past. When she did, he arrested her with his hands around her shoulders, pinning her to the spot. The scent of his cologne reached her and the familiarity of it made her yearn to move closer against him, to allow him to hold her, but it was a risk she couldn't take. She was too fragile.

"Let me go, I want to go home."

"I'm taking you home."

She stared at him, unsure of his meaning.

"I want you to give it a chance, we both do. Come home with us and we'll start at the beginning."

She shook her head, knowing that if she went somewhere more private, into their personal space, it would be even harder to draw a line under this. "I'm not normal, Owen. I can't even have a relationship with one man, let alone two. I have to stop now because it's getting harder and harder to protect myself."

"You don't need to protect yourself any more. I'm here to protect you. Alec, too."

Frustration doubled up inside her. "You don't understand what my life is like, no one does."

"We will. We're trying. I'm warning you, we're tenacious bastards, both of us, and we want more of you."

How good that sounded, and how much it scared her. *I want to go with him.*

Monica glanced away and looked up at Cumbernauld's. It was her place, her rock, or it had been, for so long. But all of that had changed and she was on the outside now. It became starkly apparent to her that she'd relied on this place too much. It was wrong to feel as if whole world fell apart, just because things weren't as she assumed at her place of work.

Most of all she knew that wasn't why she wanted to go with him. She wanted to go with him because this was the chance of everything she thought she'd never be able to have, a loving relationship. It might be split between two men, but in an odd way that worked, for them all.

His hands were still locked on her shoulders

What if I fail them? What if I can't cope? "It'll be too hard." She glanced back at him, pleading with him to help her sort it out. She needed his control, his discipline in her crazy world.

"We'll take it slowly. It won't be too much pressure because there are three of us. Monica, we've been looking for you. We want you to be our third."

She saw the honesty in his eyes, the belief. He really wanted this. He thought it could work. "You've only known me for four days, how can you be sure?"

"We're willing to work at this."

"I'm scared that I won't be able to be what you want."

A wry smile flitted across his handsome face. He drew her closer. "Put your hands on my chest."

She shook her head and attempted to pull free.

"Monica, put your hands on my chest." He spoke deliberately, forbidding her to disobey.

Every part of her yearned for him, for his instinct and the measured control that helped her make sense of her strange, isolated world. But she couldn't put her hands on his chest, because he was such an intense man. She didn't want to learn things about him that would spoil the memory of what they'd had. "I can't. Let me just remember it as it was."

"That's not enough, and you know it. Give us a chance." He moved his hands down her arms to her wrists. "Give yourself a chance."

Still her instinct was to turn away, to pull free of his grip and run. When he drew her hands up to his chest, her fingers curled into fists.

But Owen wasn't having any of that. He gently eased his thumbs into her palms, massaging his way, opening her up, then he took her hands flat to his chest, fingers splayed. "Look at me."

Monica shook her head, attempting to pull back. Doubt assailed her. But then she felt it. Even before her hands made contact with his jacket—even when they were still an inch from him—the energy and emotions funneled towards her arrested her attention, making her falter.

Owen locked her hands there.

Images flashed through her mind, images of herself in orgasm. Entwined with that was the immense pleasure and pride he felt in bringing her to that point. With an astonished cry, she met his gaze.

He nodded. "When you touched my lips last night, it wasn't negative. I had to try this to stop you running away."

Monica nodded, remembering. Her heart hammered in her chest, and she realized how cautious he'd been, how caring and how determined. A knot of emotion built in her chest. Then he encouraged her, and she moved her fingers inside his jacket and splayed them on his shirt. There she could feel the warm heat of his body through the fabric, and she opened herself fully to it.

She felt his joy, the deep longing he had to be with her, as images of their time together flashed through her mind. She had never seen herself away before and it astonished her. *This man cares about me. Really cares*.

"Owen, oh, Owen, hold me." She moved her hands, but only so that she could press herself closer against him. Her fingers locked on his shoulders, and she clung to him, her face against his chest where she could feel his heart beating.

A moment later he lifted her chin. "Let me put this out there right now. If you ever experience my memories of other woman, all that you'll see is that not one of them ever compared to you." He smiled and took her hand to his mouth, resting a kiss on her splayed fingers. "We want you to be our woman."

Dizzy with emotion and weak with gratitude, she clutched at his lapel, the wet leather slippery under her fingers. She blinked. Her vision was being obscured by rain. *Not crying*.

Owen kissed her cheekbone—kissed away those tears. "As you may have noticed," he added, "we like a challenge, and you're it, Monica Evans."

"Owen…" It was all she could muster, but it was enough.

"Come on, Alec is waiting in the car, we're going home." He put his arm around her shoulder and turned her to the curb. For the first time she noticed that a black limousine was parked nearby, idling, the wipers constantly swiping away the rain.

As they approached the door opened, and she saw Alec waited inside.

A uniformed chauffeur was at the wheel, hived off by a mirrored glass wall.

Alec had been watching. He'd been waiting for her too. She felt weak with relief, and when he put out his hand to her, Monica didn't hesitate. She took it.

Chapter Fourteen

The noise from the outside world was muted, making the luxurious limousine the perfect place for her to catch her breath and address the step she had just taken. The interior lights were low, and the faint sound of music only just reached them from sound system. And the two men who were with her watched over her adoringly.

Monica felt buoyant, surreal, and yet she was growing mellow, too.

She rested her head on Alec's shoulder, savoring the way his shoulder felt against her face and body. As they traveled through London, the images outside the window blurred together in the rainy night and she let the comfortable interior of the limousine soothe her. Whatever happened, happened. They had convinced her and she was going to give it a go. The sense of liberation that she experienced after making that decision was unbelievable. It was as if a huge weight had been lifted from her, a weight which she had been carrying for so long. The truth of it was she was a woman and she needed fulfillment. She had to pursue the chance for happiness, and if they were willing to give it a go she shouldn't fight it, not any more.

After they'd been driving for a while, Owen latched his hand around the back of her knees and swung her legs so that they were across his lap. He took off her high-heeled shoes and massaged her toes through her stockings. She chuckled softly when he tickled her. With her upper body cocooned by Alec's embrace, and Owen's attention to her feet, she wondered if she was dreaming.

"You're wet through," she commented as she looked at Owen.

"I've got a big tub at home. Big enough for three."

Somehow she could have guessed that. "No kidding."

"Maybe I can convince you to scrub my back."

"Maybe you can." She felt a bit like a stray kitten they'd picked up in the street and were taking back to their place. Maybe she was. The strangeness of the day was giving way to hope, curiosity and anticipation.

"Where are you taking me? Where is it that you live?" There was so much about them that she didn't know. It was so odd, the way life unfolded. She felt so close to these two men, and yet there was so much more to explore. It suddenly occurred to her that if he was a new member of the Board of Directors—and Jack Monroe's son—his home might be in Switzerland.

"Hampstead. I have a house there."

That was a relief. Her curiosity was up and running.

"Do you live together?" She knew they slept together and worked together, but she didn't know what their living arrangements were.

Alec ran his fingers through her hair and kissed her forehead before he responded. "I have a place of my own, a flat by the river."

"He also has a key to my place." Owen smiled at her.

"Do you two ever kiss?"

She'd never seen them kiss. She'd seen plenty of other intimate contact, but it made her curious that she hadn't seen that. Perhaps they didn't kiss. If that was true, it was a real shame.

Alec grinned. "You were right," he said to Owen, "she really is into man-on-man." He prodded her with an accusing finger. "Pervert."

Monica chuckled. "You look really hot together. I can't help it if I like to see it."

She thought about that, looking from one to the other of them, picturing it. She didn't have to picture it for long. Alec leant over and wrapped his hand around the back of Owen's head. Before he moved in, Owen shot her a smoldering glance. Then his mouth was on Alec's, his arms wrapped around his lover's neck as they kissed, right there in front of her.

Monica stared, loving the way they looked, and when Alec thrust his tongue into Owen's mouth her core clenched, the need to grind down onto the seat—or preferably a willing erection—gripping her. When they drew apart a moment later, Owen ducked his head and gave Alec a play-bite on the jaw. That these two were very familiar with kissing one another was obvious.

Owen sat back and resumed his attention to her feet. "Happy now?"

His eyes twinkled when he asked the question. It had amused him greatly that she'd asked that.

She shrugged. "I wouldn't mind seeing some more."

"Oh, you will." He moved his thumbs over the balls of her feet, stimulating her nerve endings and making the tiny muscles in her feet bliss out.

She nodded at the mirrored divide between them and the driver. "I assume the driver can't see what's going on in here."

"Yes, he can," Alec replied, "in fact he begs to drive us around all day so he can see what we get up to. He's a pervert, much like you."

Monica laughed and the remaining tension faded away as she basked in their presence. "You are kidding, right?"

"He's kidding," Owen replied. "The driver can't see what's going on here."

When she looked into his eyes, she had the strange feeling that he didn't really care if he was seen. It made sense. Owen was sure and happy in his self, which meant that he didn't need to worry about what other people thought. She doubted he made a big song and dance about who he slept with, he was discreet in all things, but he wouldn't shy away from it. Instinctively she knew that.

"How much of a pervert are you?" Owen added, and that wicked smile of his was back. "I think we need to know, don't you, Alec?"

"Yes, I think you should confess." Alec kissed her neck while he spoke, his breath hot against her tender skin on her throat.

Monica attempted to feign an innocent expression. It was hard with so much male testosterone surrounding her and the potential for hot sex imminent.

Alec moved in against her ear, kissed her there then whispered. "How about a bit of man-on-man-on-woman? Do you think you could handle that?"

Monica pictured it, and her body responded instantly. The simmering arousal she felt turned quickly into a blazing inferno of desire. She squirmed on her seat and her head dropped back against Alec's shoulder.

"We'll take that as a sign of interest then, shall we?" Alec teased.

Moments later the limousine pulled in at a beautiful Georgian town house.

Monica climbed out of the car and looked at the place. It was familiar to her, and she knew why. While Alec opened the door to the house, she recalled the early images that she'd seen when she'd handled his keys. She touched the door as she passed. This was Owen's home.

It was a palatial house and when she stood in the hallway with her coat and bag clutched in her hand, she felt suddenly unprepared. Alec took her damp coat and arranged it on the back of a chair. Then he was back at her side, embracing her easily as if there was nothing he enjoyed more. The way he foiled her body, standing behind her and stroking her hip bones while he kissed her neck, made her feel safe again and she savored it. "It's been such a weird day. This means a lot to me, you bringing me here."

Owen closed the gap between them. "This is just the beginning." He stared at her, looking deep into her eyes, daring her to defy that comment.

With a trembling intake of breath, she nodded.

At her back, Alec growled possessively.

Owen reached into his pocket, and pulled out a set of handcuffs.

"Oh, they are beautiful." Monica stared at them, entranced. They were delicately made, and when he held them up to the light, she saw that the slender metal wristbands were engraved with her name.

Owen smiled, and closed his hand over the cuffs, keeping them there in the palm of his hand. Desire fluttered in the pit of her belly.

"So, would you like to see the kitchen first, or the bedroom?" He lifted an eyebrow. "As house guest you get to decide."

"Sex first, then food," she replied, without hesitation. The need to seal her commitment to them was urgent.

"Good choice," Alec said.

Owen rested his hand around her waist and led her up the marble staircase.

She moved as if walking through a dream, but she knew it was real. It struck her again how sensitive he was about her issues with touch. The logical thing would have been to go for her hand, but he remembered. She knew it took effort. It took effort on her own part, and this was new to them. Would she ever be able to show them just how much that meant to her? She was sure as hell going to try.

Owen's bedroom was large, spacious and yet understated. There were amber colored blinds on the windows which warmed the streetlight they let into the room. A Tiffany lamp by the bed was the only obvious decadence.

The bed itself was huge, but she kind of expected that from him.

Alec began to undress her, and she felt deliriously happy, like it was the most natural thing in the world to stand there as he disrobed her, while Owen watched. High on the moment, she could barely take her eyes off the pair of them to look at her surroundings.

Alec unlatched her bra, casting it aside. Then he reached around from behind and lifted her breasts and hands, rubbing his fingers over the peaked nipples as if offering them to Owen. It made her hips roll, and when Owen's gaze dropped to look at her chest, she lifted one foot from the ground, barely able to stand still because of the intense desire spiraling inside her. The heady atmosphere was enchanting, the shift in their relationship that the day had brought about spinning magic through each and every moment. She felt drunk on it.

Owen unbuttoned his shirt and took it off. He approached with the handcuffs in his hand and she instinctively put her wrists out for him. When he slid the slender cuffs around her wrists, the muscles in his chest and upper arms rippled, and the sight of his gorgeous body naked and flexing made her ache for contact.

While Owen secured the cuffs, Alec dropped to a squat behind her and drew her undies down the length of her legs. When they were off, he slid his fingers into the juncture between her thighs and stroked her right there in the hot niche of her pussy.

She was so wet that his thumb slid easily inside her, and he unfurled one finger pushed it between her thighs and rested it over her clit. When she moaned with pleasure, he blew across the backs of her thighs, which made her legs tremble under her. She felt him brush the back of her thigh and he kissed her there, so she glanced back at him and saw that his eyes were bright with suggestion as he looked up at her.

Owen clicked the cuffs shut. "I think Alec wants to fuck you."

Monica's heart tripped. Her attention went from one to the other and when she looked back down Alec, he nodded and there was a slight pout to his lips. He had not yet penetrated her that way, and she sensed that he'd been biding his time, waiting for Owen to indicate it was the right moment. Was that it, Owen would only share the ultimate act of intimacy once he was sure this was moving forward? Breathless, fascinated and massively aroused, she marveled at the subtle symbiosis between them.

Alec moved his thumb slowly, exploring her opening, and when he stretched her open suggestively the idea of having his cock there ricocheted through her senses, making her need urgent.

"I'd like that, I'd like that a lot," she managed to respond.

Alec eased his thumb out and for a moment he sucked on it, his eyes filled with mischief. She laughed softly and Owen latched his hand over the chain between her cuffed wrists, and led her to the bed.

Owen patted the bed, and she sat down then laid out on it as he directed, allowing him to guide her with a tug on the cuffs. When she was comfortable he moved her cuffed hands above her head, resting them safely between two pillows. He then arranged another pillow beneath her shoulders, and looked her over as if assuring himself of her comfort. She felt treasured, wanted, and cared for.

Each moment was precious and she savored it, almost afraid that she'd wake up back on that bed in the hotel room at Cumbernauld's, where she'd felt as if her whole world was crumbling. Instead, she was here, on the brink of something that was entirely possible because they wanted to make it so.

More than anything, she wanted them both. She wanted everything—every combination and every decadence that their relationship offered. She knew they would protect her from too much when it mattered, and she trusted them with that.

When he was undressed, Alec stood at the side of the bed and rolled a rubber onto his erection. He was more serious than he had been before, and she could tell he'd been anticipating this. How unnerving, how rewarding. All the things they had already done together flitted through her mind, and her hips lifted and rolled against the bed.

Alec climbed over her and between her legs. He kissed her mouth, his hands caressing her sides, his thumbs stroking the soft skin beneath her breasts. "I've been longing to do this."

The weight and pressure of his erection against the seam of her pussy and her swollen clit was too good. "I'm ready."

A fleeting smile crossed his face as he directed his cock to her opening, easing it inside. The feeling of him stretching her open made her cuffed wrists lift from their nest between the pillows and her body arched. She put her feet flat to the bed, drawing her knees up, inviting him in.

Then she saw Owen.

Nothing could have prepared her for the intensity of having Alec enter her, while Owen watched from beyond. She could see the possessive look burning in his eyes, but it was possessive of both of them. The pleasure he took in seeing them united this way was deeply special to him, something she wondered if he'd ever approved before.

"Oh, yes, you feel so good," Alec whispered, as he thrust the length of his erect cock inside her. He arched over her, weight balanced on his elbows as his hips thrust back and forth in a slow, seductive rhythm. A moment later she gasped and caught her bottom lip between her teeth because he smiled and paused to grind his hips deep against her centre, sensitizing her core to the max. She whimpered aloud, the skin all over her body prickling.

He began to thrust again and buried his head at her neck, kissing her and licking her skin. The stimulation made her arch from the bed so that she could press her peaked nipples against the hard wall of his chest, making them sting. Pleasure looped through her, and when her eyes locked with Owen's, she felt her world click into place as surely as the cuffs he had clicked round her wrists.

He nodded at her, as if he knew. When he moved, it was with deliberation. He rolled a condom onto his cock and reached for the lube. With quick moves he climbed over Alec's back. Alec groaned under the ministrations of Owen's fingers. Then Owen leaned in to kiss her mouth, with Alec between them. Breathlessly, she kissed him, eager and yet surprised at the action. When he drew back, a smile flitted over his face. "Ready?"

She nodded.

Then Alec lifted his head, and his face contorted, as she knew that Owen was driving himself inside Alec.

"Oh my God." She felt it all, because the response echoed in Alec's cock inside her. Already long and hard, it seemed to swell and lift when he was penetrated, rubbing against the front wall of her sex. Then Owen began to thrust, and the intensity of the chain reaction swept her away.

She could no longer think straight, she could only react and respond, as her hips arched to take the double pressure of man on man on her. Each thrust sent a flurry of wild sensation hurtling through her groin—and they had lots to give her.

The visceral force of the two men forced wave after wave of stimulation through her core. Pressure built, like a hot rock lodged in her womb, waiting to roll free. While they worked her, her core began to clutch and spasm, the tight nub of her clit thrumming wildly every time Alec crushed against it.

She cried out and when she did Owen reached to clasp her side, holding onto her as his movements sped.

"Monica," Alec whispered, and she could see who was about to come—she could feel it too. Her core clamped hard onto Alec's cock as he climaxed and release rolled over her.

She was still shuddering, still adrift, when she saw that Owen was close, his eyes locked on hers, his lips parted. Every muscle in his body was taut with effort. Then he cursed below his breath, his movement suddenly slowing to a stop as he hit his peak.

Hours later, after they had eaten, bathed in the tub, and lingered over wine and snacks, they took her back to bed. She knew they had plotted something, she knew they'd whispered together when they'd gone to collect the drinks and food. The knowledge made her nervous. When they returned, she sat up against the pillows and they laid either side of her.

At first they chatted about Flynn Elwood and Sheila Trent, and how unlikely it was. "I met his wife once, and she struck me as the sort of woman who had her own interests, but still it's got to hurt, if she had no clue."

Alec nodded. "I wondered what she was like. It's a difficult one to call, but maybe it's better she found out now, rather than later."

They discussed the subject for some time and through chatting about someone else's relationship it gave Monica enough space to deal with what was happening here. At the back of her mind she wondered about Owen. This house—was this his home? If he was on the Board of Directors, didn't that mean he lived in Switzerland? Eventually she plucked up the courage to ask. “If this is your home, does that mean you’re based in England?”

He nodded. “At the current time, yes. My parents are both British but they live in Geneva. I went to school and to university in England, and my first job for the Board was working on hotel chain here, so I made myself a base here.”

“Which hotel chain?” The curiosity she felt about all that was yet unknown to her about them lifted her spirits, and it all felt a little less strange. She began to feel as if it was real, and she was more grounded.

“The Royal Blue Standards.” He watched for her reaction when he said that.

“I heard about that, was that you?” She laughed softly when he nodded. “I should have known!” The Royal Blue Standards was a chain of country house hotels overseen by the same Board of Directors. It had a long history and a top pedigree, but the buildings had become a bit decrepit for the price they charged and the prevailing attitude was rather staid. The hotels had undergone huge changes over the past three years. “I heard that someone had been drafted in to haul it into the twenty-first century. “

Alec gave a sideways nod at their companion. “That would be Owen here.”

Owen shrugged off the remark. “The Royal Blues was a test for me. I succeeded, so I had a chance to move up. Call it work experience.” He flashed her a grin. “I have to overhaul the entire Cumbernauld’s chain to secure my place on the Board.”

“All over the world?”

“Yep. The Royal Blues was a great try out. Twenty country house hotels in the UK, next up Cumbernauld’s. Thirty-two hotels in fourteen different countries, worldwide.”

She stared at him, taking onboard how different his life was. Did this mean that he would be leaving London soon, despite his suggestion of a more long-term relationship?

Don't let it faze you, she urged herself, unwilling to lose sight of the dream. It was hard to ignore it though.

A moment later she looked Alec. "Did you work together at The Royal Blues?"

She asked question mainly to distract herself from where her thoughts were wandering. Already the talk of them moving on had taken hold of her and was squeezing her insides.

"Yes. That's where I first got hitched up with trouble here." Alec winked. "It was an immense project, each hotel with its own set of issues, but nothing like what lies ahead. It's going to be exciting." Anticipation glowed in his eyes.

"I bet." The three of them had so much in common, she realized, working in the hotel trade. At first she'd assumed them PR people, then private investigators. Now she knew the full story.

Owen looked at her thoughtfully. "Alec was assigned to me as a temporary measure, but we worked so well together it continued. I kept Alec with me not just because I enjoy his company and I care for him, but because I could see how good he was at his job. That's the kind of thing I do."

He stared at her rather deliberately.

"So, where do you go from here, with your work?" She asked it tentatively, almost scared to hear him say they would be leaving London.

"I have to make a full report to headquarters tomorrow, which I can do by webcam. Then we'll make a schedule of changes and developments for Cumbernauld's of London, now that we've unearthed the source of the problems. We'll see if the Board approve the changes I suggest."

"Changes?"

"We'll have to put a new management system in place, new personnel." He studied her intently as he spoke.

"Maybe a new housekeeping manager, if I can convince you to jump ship."

She did a double take. "What are you trying to say?"

"Think what a great team we'd make, the three of us."

She could see he was serious by his expression, but it was so unexpected she didn't know how to react.

Alec rested his fingers on her arm. "Owen is right. We would make a great team. We'd take on the world, and think about how much fun we would have, after hours."

His reaction was important. Whilst Owen appeared to be the more grounded of the two, it was Alec who made sure Owen didn't get ahead of himself, she could see that. If Alec thought it might work, could she believe it too?

Owen was determined to convince her. "Alec and I have worked really well together because we trust each other on a personal level too. The task ahead is much bigger than The Royal Blue Standard chain revamp. It's a worldwide task; it would demand high levels of research and engagement with the staff at each hotel. That means I need more personnel who I can really trust…think about it. If you work with us, we can protect you all the time. And you would be valued, highly valued."

"But…" Alas, she couldn't think of a good excuse.

Owen reached over and put his finger to her lips. The erotic buzz she got from that made her chuckle, and she pulled his hand away. "You're going to keep pulling that stunt on me, aren't you?"

"Of course I am." Affection glowed in his eyes. "Seriously, you would be such an asset to this team. You helped us uncover the problems here in London branch."

"No way. It was only a matter of time before you found out. You knew that Flynn had to be involved, somehow, that's why you wouldn't accept his suggestion of who to work with in the first place."

"That's true," he responded in a matter of fact manner. There was no smugness there whatsoever. "But you made things move quicker. Your psychic skill is something you currently keep under wraps, and…it makes you afraid of life."

He paused.

She nodded. He was right.

"We can see that it's been a burden. If you join us it could be a real asset to you, and to us."

"Is that why you want me?"

"No. You know it isn't. I wanted you before that. The psychic stuff is a bonus, but I'd be making this proposal either way. You have a terrific resume, and you're a loyal employee. You are thorough, and you understand the Cumbernauld's ethos more than any member of staff I've ever met."

Pride blossomed in her chest. His words meant a lot to her.

"If you take us up on this, your life would be different. If things ever got too tough for you because of your psychometrics we've got each other, you could take time out."

That made her heart ache. He'd thought it through, every angle. Owen Clifford went after what he wanted and she saw it now, clear as day. He wanted her. Affection, desire, and a sound business proposal had all played their part. The sensitivity with which he spoke about her secret psychic self was the real seal on the deal.

"Monica, please think about it. And when I say that I mean I want you to take time, think about it over the next few days while we're looking at the future of Cumbernauld's of London, then give me any good reasons why not. I promise I'll hear you out."

She went to respond, but he shook his head. She lifted her hands in surrender. "Okay, I'll think about it."

"Good, now let's stop talking."

Monica stared at him. He really meant it. Then she saw the humor in his yes. Owen and Alec looked at each other across her. With a silent agreement, they each held her around one wrist and cradled her hand inside one of theirs. Her palms were facing up, vulnerable and exposed. She trembled, and for a fleeting moment she wondered if they were testing her ability to relax with them.

But they weren't.

Owen exchanged glances with Alec, then they both kissed her in the palms of her hand.

"Oh!" Her arms jerked, the old familiar reticence seizing her.

They didn't let her break free.

The nerve endings in her hands and forearms vibrated, because their actions loosed a flurry of sensation through her palms, up her arms, into her body.

"Owen?" She looked at him pleadingly.

There was a smile on his lips when he lifted his head. "Let us explore you."

They had plotted this, and they were forcing her to enjoy. Between gentle brushes of their lips and their hot breath on her skin, she felt their mutual desire for her, the urge to possess and nurture that had evolved between the three of them.

"I'm still scared," she blurted.

"We know." Owen's voice soothed her.

Each touch they made coursed through her, each point of contact opening up a cornucopia of images in her mind—images of them together and desiring her, images of their first kisses, images of tonight. All of it rolled together through her mind and body and she undulated against the bed, her body riding high on the experience.

"Don't fight it," Owen instructed in a husky whisper.

Her heart brimmed with emotion. “I won’t, not anymore.”

Instead Monica pressed her head back against the pillows. In the cocoon of their affection she embraced her secret, closed her eyes, and allowed herself to enjoy.

*

ABOUT THE AUTHOR

Saskia Walker is an award-winning British author of erotic fiction. Her short stories and novellas have appeared in over one hundred international anthologies including Best Women's Erotica, The Mammoth Book of Best New Erotica, Secrets, and Wicked Words. Her erotica has also been featured in several international magazines including Cosmo, Penthouse, Bust, and Scarlet. Fascinated with seduction, Saskia loves to explore how and why we get from saying "hello" to sharing our most intimate selves in moments of extreme passion. After writing shorts for several years Saskia moved into novel-length projects. Her erotic single titles include The Burlington Manor Affair, Rampant, Reckless and the Taskill Witches trilogy: The Harlot, The Libertine and The Jezebel. Her novels Double Dare and Rampant both won Passionate Plume awards and her writing has twice been nominated for a RT Book Reviews Reviewers' Choice Award. Nowadays Saskia is happily settled in Yorkshire, in the north of England, with her real-life hero, Mark, and a houseful of stray felines. You can visit her website for more info. www.saskiawalker.co.uk

If you enjoyed this novel you might enjoy HOLLY'S INTUITION, book two in the Erogenous Zones series – a contemporary erotic ménage romance series about three sisters who have psychic abilities, and the very special men who love them.

Holly's neighbours, Joshua and Stewart, are fit, gorgeous, and gay – or that's what she thinks. Then one day, after coming to his aid following an accident, she forms a deep connection with Joshua, and subsequently becomes a psychic voyeur into his love life with Stewart. Holly has never experienced anything so intense, erotic, and arousing before, and despite her confusion about why this has happened to her, she can think of little else but being in the bed with the two men.

Joshua is trying to come to terms with being gay, and he's about to announce his sexuality to his family. But now Holly has entered the scene and he's drawn to her as well as to his partner, Stewart. Since his accident he feels close to Holly. She calms him…and arouses him. Sharing Stewart with her shouldn't be this much of a turn-on, but it is.

Stewart is bisexual, and his attraction to Holly is something he's been keeping under wraps for the sake of his relationship -- until he discovers Joshua is attracted to her as well. When they end up in a threesome, sex has never been this hot, but Joshua is even more confused about his sexuality as a result. Then Holly confides her psychic ability, adding a whole new dimension that none of them can ignore. Her intuition has brought them together, but will it also tear them apart?

Available now in print and digital format.

Visit www.saskiawalker.co.uk for more details on Saskia's other works. Thank you for reading!